Mills & Boon
Best Seller Romance

A chance to read and collect some of the best-loved novels from Mills & Boon—the world's largest publisher of romantic fiction.

Every month, six titles by favourite Mills & Boon authors will be re-published in the *Best Seller Romance* series.

A list of other titles in the *Best Seller Romance* series can be found at the end of this book.

Lilian Peake

PASSIONATE INVOLVEMENT

MILLS & BOON LIMITED
LONDON · TORONTO

All the characters in this book have no existence outside the imagination of the Author, and have no relation whatsoever to anyone bearing the same name or names. They are not even distantly inspired by any individual known or unknown to the Author and all the incidents are pure invention.

The text of this publication or any part thereof may not be reproduced or transmitted in any form or by any means, electronic or mechanical, including photocopying, recording, storage in an information retrieval system, or otherwise without the written permission of the publisher.

This book is sold subject to the condition that it shall not by way of trade or otherwise, be lent, resold, hired out or otherwise circulated without the prior consent of the publisher in any form of binding or cover other than that in which it is published and without a similar condition including this condition being imposed on the subsequent purchaser.

First published 1977
Australian copyright 1983
Philippine copyright 1983
This edition 1983

© Lilian Peake 1977

ISBN 0 263 74309 8

Set in Linotype Plantin 10 on 11 pt.
02-0583

Made and printed in Great Britain by
Richard Clay (The Chaucer Press) Ltd,
Bungay, Suffolk

CHAPTER ONE

The taxi braked to a halt, deposited its passenger and her luggage on the pavement and went on its way. Tamsin paused to read the name which was carved down the stone columns to which the entrance gates were attached. Hotel Tranquillité, it said.

'Peace and quiet, that's what you need, dear,' her uncle had remarked when her convalescence had ended. 'You'll find them at one of my hotels. I own a handful in the British Isles, as you know. But you can take your pick of Europe—France, Holland, Italy or Switzerland. I've got a hotel in each.'

He really was her rich uncle, not an imaginary one. He was her Uncle William, her father's amply-built, grey-haired brother. He was good-natured but hard-headed, an unusual kind of businessman who was shrewd and exacting but humane, too. Tamsin preferred her own father, of course—a quiet, retiring kind of man, the complete opposite of his brother, although she had a special corner in her heart reserved for her Uncle William.

Of all the places in which Uncle William had owned hotels, Tamsin had chosen Switzerland. It was a place which she had longed since childhood to visit. And now here she was, by the shores of Lake Lugano, where she had arranged to stay for a while after recovering from a road accident.

It had happened when she had been cycling home from the town. A car had swung out of a side road. The driver had been talking to his front seat passenger and had not paused, as he should have done, at the junction of the two roads. It had been Tamsin's misfortune to be moving across the driver's path.

The car had knocked her from her bicycle and as she had hit the surface of the road she had blacked out for a few moments. It was lucky, people had told her afterwards, that there had been nothing coming in the opposite direction, otherwise everything could have been so much worse.

As it was, she had sustained concussion, considerable areas of bruising and grazing of the skin where she had scraped along the ground for a short distance. It had also been necessary to insert a few stitches into a wound at the side of her head. She had been kept in hospital overnight, but had been discharged next day to be looked after by her anxious parents.

As she convalesced, she had considered her uncle's suggestion. It would be pleasant, she had decided, to be pampered a little in surroundings bordering on luxury. All of her uncle's hotels, she knew, had been designated by those who knew about such things—travel agents, tour operators and so on—as being in the first-class category. Which meant that only those with a healthy bank balance could afford to spend their vacations within their costly walls.

Carrying her cases, Tamsin walked up the sloping drive, passing a blue, sunflecked swimming pool filled with people. At the foot of the short flight of steps leading up to the main entrance of the hotel, she paused again. At first, she saw only the façade of the hotel, with its many floors, its balconies painted white and the walls painted red.

All this, she told herself with pride, belonged to her uncle. Well, she had to be honest, not entirely. He was chairman of the company which owned it, together with a number of other hotels spread across Europe.

It was then that she noticed the man who stood at the top of the flight of steps. There could be no doubt Tamsin thought, that *his* bank balance was healthy! It was all there in his self-confident pose as he leant against the door frame;

in his attitude as he stood, thumbs hooked into the belt around his waist; in the arrogant look in his eyes which put him into the 'first-class category', like the hotel whose guest he almost certainly was.

Even allowing for the angle at which Tamsin stared at him, his height seemed formidable. This she could judge by comparing him with other men who passed in and out of the building. She had a hazy impression of jet black hair and tanned skin beneath a pale lemon shirt, partly unbuttoned. His slacks were dark and close-fitting, his feet, which were crossed at the ankles, pushed into expensive-looking sandals.

There was about him a look of remoteness, the aloofness of an aristocrat ... He seemed to be looking inward, absorbed in his thoughts, but unexpectedly his eyes shifted and he was gazing narrowly at the girl at the foot of the steps as she gazed up at him.

Embarrassed, Tamsin jerked her eyes downwards and bent to pick up her suitcases.

'*Halten Sie! Bleiben Sie dort!*' It seemed the guest was German. Since Tamsin could not understand the language, she braced herself and tightened her hold on the cases.

'*Attendez! Restez là!*' Astonished, Tamsin stared up at the man. French now!

'I—I'm sorry,' she faltered, 'I——'

'So you're English. Wait there a moment.' The man had lifted himself upright from the door frame. His tone was imperious, telling of an autocrat behind the relaxed manner.

The man looked over his shoulder through the glass doors leading into the hotel. '*Facchino!*' There was no response.

'It really doesn't matter,' Tamsin called, self-effacingly. 'I'm used to carrying my own baggage. I——' I'm not the usual kind of hotel guest, she wanted to tell him. I'm just my uncle's niece and he's being kind and paying for me ... She knew how ridiculous it would sound.

'Wait a moment,' the command came again, 'I'm calling for the porter.'

Tamsin shook her head. 'It's all right. I——' Her voice tailed off. How could she tell this man that with her modest family background she was used to doing everything for herself? Politeness forced her to wait for a few seconds to see if the man's call was answered, but no one came. As she started up the steps the man made a sharp comment in yet another language which she could not understand—could it have been Italian?—and he came down the steps towards her.

'No, thank you,' she said again, guessing his intention. 'I told you, I'm used to——'

'There's no need for you to carry your luggage yourself.' He was facing her now, standing one step above her, and she could see in detail what she had only glimpsed from the distance. Her gaze skimmed over a long, tanned throat and a jutting, determined chin. She noted the straight classical nose, the black hair which matched in colour the miniature jungle which sprawled on his chest and which the unfastened buttons revealed.

Now, in close-up, Tamsin could discern no warmth in his eyes, only a cool, male assessment of her potential as a female. There was no doubting the experience of those thick-browed eyes, and she bristled at the man's unmistakable classification of her as an inferior specimen of her sex.

His next words surprised her, but they were spoken without compassion. 'You look tired from your journey.'

Despite herself, Tamsin felt a curious stirring of disappointment. Was that all he had seen as a result of his scrutiny of her features? At home she had boy-friends, two or three in fact, who had been students at the college of education like herself. If they had not found her wanting in attractiveness, why should this man dismiss her merely as an object to be pitied instead of admired?

The unfortunate and discomfiting thing was that a mere

searching look from those two keen brown eyes only a short distance above her had been sufficient to remind her that she was a very feminine animal with all the normal, primitive desire to appear attractive to the opposite sex.

She was tired from nearly twenty-four hours of travelling, including a night spent in a rocking, rather bumpy couchette. 'Of course I'm not tired,' she bluffed, and made as if to pass him and go on her way.

He moved and put himself in her path. A slight smile lifted the corners of his mouth. 'With a fit, able-bodied male available on the doorstep, why should any attractive young woman carry her own cases?' His tone was sardonic as he looked her over. He smiled but his eyes remained cool. His lips, she noticed with a shock—she had never looked so closely at a man's lips before—were well-shaped and full, with a suggestion of sensuality about them. Tamsin realised with a skip of her heartbeats how good-looking he was.

'Please,' she said, 'would you let me pass?'

'Your cases.' It seemed he was determined not to move until he had his way. Seconds later they were securely in his grasp and he was making his way upward. 'Follow me,' he said, and she had no choice but to obey.

By the time they had reached the top of the steps the porter had appeared. He swept open the glass door and bowed them in. Judging by his expression, he spoke apologetically in Italian to the man who carried the cases. The porter bent to take the cases, but the man motioned him away.

With the suitcases still in his hands, the man turned to Tamsin. 'I assume you've booked a room?'

'Yes, I—my——' Tamsin stopped. *Don't tell them who you are, dear,* her uncle had said. *It would be a good opportunity for me to check up first hand on how the hotel's being managed.*

'You mean act as a *spy*?' Tamsin had asked, horrified.

Her uncle had laughed, but there had been a thoughtful look on his face. 'It sounds bad put like that,' he'd said. 'But you'd be doing me a good turn, lass. If I stayed in one of my own hotels, they'd know, wouldn't they, and put everything right in advance, like they do when royalty goes anywhere.'

Tamsin had had to agree that his statement had been reasonable.

'Your——?' the man was saying, looking surprised at her hesitation in answering his question. 'Your room—you have reserved one?' he repeated, a little impatiently.

'Yes, yes, I have,' she hastened to tell him. She certainly could not say, 'My uncle's secretary reserved it for me.'

The man stopped at the reception desk and put down the two suitcases, motioning Tamsin to the desk. He did not go, however, but lingered nearby.

The receptionist smiled. 'Your name, madam?' Her English accent was good, but it was plain that her true nationality was Italian. Tamsin took a breath. This would be the test.

'Selby,' she said and held her breath.

The receptionist nodded, showing not even the faintest flicker of surprise.

'What name shall I use?' Tamsin had asked her uncle. 'If I use my real name, won't they know it's the same as yours?'

'It's doubtful,' her uncle had replied. 'I'm the chairman of the company and employees as far away as they are wouldn't be familiar with individual names.'

Her uncle had been right. To the receptionist the name did not strike even a spark of recognition. 'You have booked a single room, Miss Selby?' The girl frowned as she consulted the list.

Tamsin swallowed. 'Actually, I——' She floundered. How could she explain away the apparent mistake?

The man who had carried her cases strolled to the desk

and leant on it on his elbow. He spoke rapidly in Italian to the receptionist, who pointed to a number and looked puzzled. The man leant across and read the number, then turned to Tamsin.

'It was a single room you wanted? It seems there's been a mistake. They've given you a double room. The receptionist says they can alter it and give you a single room. They have one free.'

A slow flush spread over Tamsin's cheeks. 'No, thank you. It's quite correct. I—er—booked a double room. I thought a single might be—well——' How could she explain it? Her ingenuity forsook her. 'Too small,' she finished lamely.

Now what had she said? The man's eyebrows rose and he looked her over with curiosity spiced with something else. Was it cynicism?

'I see,' said the receptionist, still doubtful.

If only, Tamsin thought, she had not allowed her uncle to talk her into having a larger room. 'Live a little, lass,' he'd said. 'You've just got over a nasty accident—luckily the consequences weren't worse—so have the best. Why not? It's free, a gift from me for my favourite niece, eh, John?' He had turned to his brother and sister-in-law. 'She deserves the best, doesn't she, this daughter of yours?'

Her mother had agreed wholeheartedly. 'Take the chance while it's there, love,' she had said.

Her father had shaken his head. 'I'm not so sure. If Tamsin's anything like me—and I know she is—she'd feel uncomfortable in the wrong surroundings.'

But her uncle had won the argument and here she was, Tamsin thought, having to defend a decision that had not been hers in the first place. But why defend? she thought with a touch of surprise. What did this man's opinion matter to her? He was a stranger, nothing more, someone who had helped to carry her cases. He had no more interest in her than in any other new arrival at the hotel.

Tamsin signed her name in the appropriate places and the porter materialised at her side. The receptionist spoke to him in Italian and Tamsin assumed she was telling him the number of her room.

Moments later they were in the lift. As the doors closed, Tamsin caught a glimpse of the stranger who had helped her. He was still leaning against the reception desk and watching her departure with a curiously sardonic smile. She wondered what she had done to deserve it.

The door to her room swung open, the porter put the cases on the carpet and left. Tamsin, holding her breath, stepped into the room and looked about her. 'Luxury', her uncle had called it. Heaven, she thought, a room which the famous and the rich would not—could not—scorn.

The room was large—wasn't it, after all, really meant for two?—and there were two beds. Behind the bedheads was pinewood panelling, wall lights and a radio. Between the beds was a telephone. Nearby stood a miniature refrigerator, a mini-bar, in which, it announced in four languages, were bottles of alcohol and refreshing drinks, kept icy cold to cool the overheated, thirsty palate.

Overawed, and with a feeling of wonder, Tamsin walked to the window and looked down upon the swimming pool. The room, it seemed, was situated at one corner of the hotel. Tamsin saw with delight that it possessed not just one but two balconies, running along two sides of the room. Opening on to each of the balconies were french windows and she stepped through one of them.

The view took her breath away. There, beyond the hotel buildings, was Lake Lugano, blue as the sky which was mirrored in its faintly rippling surface. Small craft and ferry boats left widening trails behind them. Green mountains rose steeply from its depths. Buildings perched on the hillsides, while all around were lush trees, shuttered villas and white-walled houses.

Tamsin became conscious that she was overdressed for

such a climate. High in the sky, the mid-afternoon sun shone, shedding warmth and well-being. For a few moments, Tamsin's tired limbs sought the comfort of one of the two yellow sun loungers. She closed her eyes and her thoughts, showing a wilfulness that dismayed her, strayed to the strange welcome she had received from the man who, on her arrival, had greeted her from the top of the hotel steps.

It was infuriating to discover how much the man remained in her mind. His English accent was perfect, his phraseology typical of a born Englishman. Yet he spoke German and French as if he had been born to those languages, too, not to mention Italian, which was the language, Tamsin was sure, in which he had murmured angrily at the porter's non-appearance.

The sun began to make its presence felt through the long sleeves of her jacket. She roused herself and went through the glass doors into the bedroom. It did not take long to empty her suitcases and fill the wardrobes. She took her cosmetics into the adjoining bathroom and arranged them on the shelf beneath the mirror which ran the length of one of the walls. A quick look at herself had her running into the bedroom and pulling off the travel-weary dress and jacket she had been wearing for so many hours.

There was, among her clothes, a floral sundress. She put it on and tied it, halter style, behind her neck. Then she started on her flyaway fair hair. The comb snagged in the neck-hugging curls and she made a face, but she soon brought her hair under some sort of control. The parting was slightly off-centre, the gently-arched brows being a little darker in colour than her hair. Below them the eyes were grey-blue and deep-set, the mouth large and inviting, the chin rounded and a perfect balance to the straight piquant nose.

Tamsin sighed, shaking her head at her reflection. If I haven't got beauty, she told herself, there's something there.

I suppose you could be kind and call it character!

But she would waste no more time staring at herself. There were many more attractive things to be looked at than the rather winsome face gazing back at her.

Behind her the bedroom door snapped shut and she walked along the corridor to descend the carpeted marble staircase which led down into the entrance foyer.

It was when her foot met the tiled floor that it came to her with a startling suddenness that she was alone in a strange land. If she went out into the sunshine, past the swimming pool and down the drive to the world beyond, she would be going in complete ignorance of the geography of the place. The street names would be meaningless, the people unfamiliar, their ways and customs foreign to her.

From the balcony outside her room, the lake had seemed almost within a hand's touch. It should surely be a simple matter to find her way to it, but what if she lost her way? This was the Italian-speaking part of Switzerland and she had no phrase book to help her.

There was no one behind the reception desk. It was not entirely deserted, however. A familiar figure leant against it, arms folded, a half-smile on his face.

In spite of herself, Tamsin's heart skipped a beat. In spite of the spontaneous and quite inexplicable animosity that watching figure aroused in her, the man's presence struck a responsive chord somewhere inside her. Annoyed with herself, she turned away from that sardonic smile. She refused to ask that man the way to anywhere.

She presented to him her bare back and shoulders and allowed her feet to take her through the doors and into the open air. The lake came into view much sooner than she had expected. A walk past apartment blocks, round a corner, along another street, down the hill and past some shops, round another corner and there it was, across the road.

All around tourists jostled. Miniature fountains set into the pavements sprayed their water in narrow artistic curves.

There were flowers, there was light, colour, sunshine and movement. It stirred in Tamsin a feeling of anticipation and excitement. This was unknown, exotic territory with —in summer, at least—a benign, indulgent climate.

There was time for leisure, for pleasure, for doing nothing at all. 'Stay as long as you want,' her uncle had said. A couple of weeks, maybe, she had thought at the time. Now she thought two *months* would hardly be long enough to savour all this ..

The lake, with its promenade and its view, called to her, but there was a formidable barrier between herself and that liquid gold-flecked expanse of blue. The passing traffic, the cars, the motor-bikes, the buses—they roared past her bewildered face in a continuous, frightening line.

Nearby was a pedestrian crossing. Tamsin walked towards it, thinking that it must surely be safe to cross there. She waited for a vehicle to stop, but it seemed she waited in vain. I'll do what everyone does at home, she thought— assume that when you put a foot on to the crossing, the oncoming car will halt.

Taking a breath—it needed courage to brave that racing, impersonal tide—she stepped on to the crossing—and cringed as a car screeched to a stop a mere arm's length away. Simultaneously a hand grabbed her arm and jerked her back on to the pavement.

'You're not in England now,' a familiar voice admonished. 'You're in a foreign land with unfamiliar ways and different values. Or was it your intention to offer yourself as a tourist martyr by flinging yourself into the rapacious jaws of the monster that goes by the name of Automobile?'

Tamsin was white and shaken and his sarcasm did nothing to calm her nerves. 'All I wanted to d-do,' she faltered, 'was to c-cross the road.'

'You had me fooled,' was the sarcastic response. 'I thought you were seeking a short cut to heaven.'

Why was he so angry with her? Why did he show no sympathy, no fellow-feeling? After all, he was English, wasn't he? Or was he? She turned her head to study him, but standing at the edge of a busy roadway was no place to do an in-depth analysis of anyone's character, let alone a man as impatient as this one appeared to be.

'It's—it's just that I'm not used to it,' she said plaintively. 'Anyway, they're all driving on the wrong—I mean, the *other* side.'

'"Wrong",' he mimicked. 'Spoken like a true Englishwoman! Whatever is different from England is "wrong".' He tutted derisively. 'How visions of the Empire linger on, even in the young!' He went on unsparingly, 'If you had wanted to cross a road as busy as this, wouldn't it have made better sense to use the underpass?' He motioned in the direction from which she had come.

She followed his eyes. 'I didn't see it,' she said in a small voice.

'Didn't *see* it? When there are notices directing you to it?'

She shook her head. 'I don't know Italian, so——'

'But you can work out symbols, surely? A drawing of steps with a figure descending?'

She sighed. He was right, of course, but he might have pointed out her error without making her feel so foolish.

She asked, partly out of curiosity, partly to make conversation as they walked from the scene of the near-accident, 'How did you know where I was?'

'I followed you.' He cut off her question with a quick, sarcastic smile. 'When you left the hotel, you seemed to be in a complete daze, in a world of your own. I felt it a pity that the hotel's newest guest should meet an untimely end in the petrol-polluted jungle that awaited her near the lakeside—where else could you have chosen to go first but to the lake?—so I decided to come after you and act as your personal protector.' He smiled, his white teeth flashing, his brown eyes becoming momentarily warm. 'Do you still want to cross the road? Shall I take your hand and lead you into the dark depths of the underpass?'

'No, thanks. I——'

With a hand on her bare shoulder—she found herself tensing unaccountably at his touch—he turned her towards him. 'Still a bit shaken? I'll buy you a coffee.' He removed his hand. Contact was broken and Tamsin felt a strange stirring of disappointment.

They walked in the direction from which they had come. The pavement was packed with tourists and the variety of foreign languages which came at her from all sides left her bewildered. The man—she still did not know his name—seemed totally unaffected by the confusion. He seemed as attuned to it as if he were an inhabitant of the place and not just another tourist.

The pavement café spilled out from the main restaurant. The tables and chairs were yellow, the awning above them striped yellow and white. 'Sit down, Miss Selby,' her companion said, pulling out a chair.

'Thank you——' She looked at him inquiringly, but he did not supply the missing name.

He sat opposite her and drummed with his fingers on the table top—again, Tamsin thought, the action of someone used to instant attention to his wishes and his demands. As he watched the passing scene, she sought in his profile for the answer to her question.

Was he English? His accent was that of an Englishman, but if that was a yardstick by which one judged his nationality, no doubt a German would consider him a German, a Frenchman would guess that he was, like himself, French.

Her eyes, covertly studying him, told her, 'No, he isn't English.' Her brain disagreed with her eyes. He's as English as you are, it told her. What, her eyes asked—with that near-black hair, those liquid brown eyes, that deeply-tanned skin?

What Englishman would do what he had done—follow her in case she had got lost, or endangered her life? Or, on such short acquaintance, taken pity on her and bought her a coffee? But his manner of speaking, his lack of hesitation over very English figures of speech...?

He turned and caught her scrutiny. Her quick colour made him smile—and it wasn't an English kind of smile. It was too warm, too sensual, too spiced with a subtle invitation. The colour in her cheeks persisted.

His eyes trailed her bare skin, lingered on her smooth shoulders, her long neck, her blonde hair. An eyebrow lifted, asking, What is it you want of me? Her colour deepened. Did he think it was *she* who was giving the invitation?

She tried to turn away from the subject which was so plainly in his mind. 'Th-thank you for—for what you did, for pulling me back when I tried to cross the road.'

He lifted a shoulder as if it was of no consequence. 'Don't let it keep you awake at night.'

There it was again, her brain said, that touch of Englishness. His teeth flashed white in a sudden smile and still her eyes said, No!

A white-jacketed waiter greeted her host as if he were an old friend. They conversed for a few moments in Italian, then her companion appeared to give an order because the waiter said, '*Si, signore*,' and went away.

'What—did you order, please?' Tamsin asked.

'Two coffees. Why, did you want something stronger?'

She shook her head vehemently.

Her companion seemed amused. 'You're a teetotaller? Have I made a *gaffe*? Do you abstain from alcoholic liquor?' He gave her a swift, smiling, sideways look. 'From all forms of pleasure, maybe? You haven't any vices, any failings? You're unblemished, virtuous—in every way?'

He was being too personal, but by the way he smiled she knew he was taunting her.

'I—I don't know your name,' she blurted out, and he threw back his head, laughing.

'So you won't give me an answer?' She was silent, sipping the hot coffee the waiter had placed in front of them. 'So why should I tell you my name?' he went on.

'You know mine,' she muttered. 'It's only fair——'

'Ah, but I only know half your name. Selby. Is that right?'

Was he delving? Did the name mean anything to him? But how could he, a guest, know of her uncle's existence? She glanced at him anxiously over the rim of her cup. Her fears were allayed. He had asked the question seriously, without the slightest hint of probing.

'Will you tell me your other name? Your first name?' His voice had taken on a softly persuasive note which any woman would find hard to resist. There was no doubt about it, this man was a practised charmer.

After a moment's hesitation, she told him.

'Tamsin.' His lips and tongue played with the name and for some strange reason her heartbeats quickened. It sounded different when spoken by him, sweeter and seasoned with intimacy ...

'A—a flight of fancy on my mother's part,' she said hastily, doing her best to suppress the colour which would give away her feelings.

'I like the name. Don't excuse it.' Now his eyes examined her over the rim of his cup. 'It suits you.' He did not qualify the statement. His cup met the saucer with a click. 'Mine's Brand, Sarne Brand.'

'Sarne? That's——'

'Unusual. So I'm constantly being told.' He smiled. 'It helps people remember me.'

'Especially women?' Now why had she said that? His way of life had absolutely nothing to do with her. She looked quickly into the brown eyes that had perceptibly hardened. 'I'm sorry. That was impertinent.'

'It was,' he replied. He did not follow the words—they were a reprimand, however softly they had been spoken—with any attempt to exonerate her for her innuendo about a side of him which was entirely his concern.

'I was named,' he went on, 'after my mother's American uncle.'

Would she now get her answer about his nationality? She asked eagerly, 'Is your mother American?'

'No. She's an Italian–Swiss. And, to save you the trouble of asking, my father was English.' Her face cleared and he laughed. 'It looks as if a piece of jigsaw has fallen into place.'

'It has, but——' She stopped, looking at him uncertainly.

'But?'

'But it's by no means finished. The—the puzzle, I mean.'

He laughed again. 'So I intrigue you? I return the compliment. How long have we got to unravel each other?'

How could she tell him how long she was staying when she didn't even know herself? 'Maybe a month.' She paused. Stay as long as you like, her uncle had said. 'Or two.'

'As long as that?' She heard the surprise. 'So you're no ordinary working girl on a couple of weeks' vacation from your job?' He looked her over with lazy eyes. He knew, Tamsin noticed, tightening with embarrassment, exactly where to start in his examination of a woman—and the places to linger.

'Strange,' he murmured. He drained the coffee from his cup, saying thoughtfully as he replaced it on the saucer, 'Let's say that I would have thought that all this'—looking around—'would be beyond your means. Not to mention such luxurious surroundings as those afforded by the Hotel Tranquillité.' He spoke the name of the hotel in meticulous French.

She traced patterns on the table-top. 'Couldn't I have

20

saved up over the months for a holiday like this?'.

'You could.' She kept her eyes down but knew he was smiling. 'Am I permitted to ask—without inviting the lash of your anger once again'—Tamsin looked at him and saw the mocking amusement—'what your work is?'

The table occupied her attention again. She paused. The admission hurt. 'I haven't got a job.'

'So,' there was a wealth of meaning in the word, 'you don't need to work for your living after all? So it seems I was wrong in my placement of you in the less wealthy part of society?'

Tamsin pressed her lips together. It was a question she would not answer. She refused to tell this man her background. Why should she tell him that, on graduating from the college of education as a teacher, there was no work awaiting her, so she had been forced to join thousands of others in the queue for teaching posts? Let him guess—and guess wrongly! What did she care? He was a guest like herself. Soon he would be gone.

'How long are you staying here?' she asked, avoiding his eyes.

'A month.' She looked at him quickly. 'Or two.' Her words. He was laughing at her. And keeping her guessing, too!

CHAPTER TWO

TAMSIN saw Sarne Brand at dinner that evening. His table was not far from hers and, like her, he sat alone.

She had taken trouble with her dressing. Not only had her uncle given her a free holiday in one of his hotels, he had insisted on giving her money with which to buy clothes.

'You're going to a luxury hotel, lass,' he'd said. 'You

must dress accordingly. You don't want to look like Cinderella amongst all those well-off, well-dressed people, do you?'

She had succumbed to her uncle's persuasion and taken the money he had offered, but only on condition that it was regarded as a loan. As soon as she had a job, she had told him, no matter what kind of job it might be, she would repay every penny. Reluctantly her uncle had agreed to her stipulation.

It was heaven to feel feminine and shapely in clothes that had not been displayed on the cheaper racks in the fashion section of the department store, but in the more expensive ranges instead. Her dress was a colourful kaftan-style pulled in at the waist with a wide belt bearing a large metal buckle. She wore no jewellery and only a light covering of make-up. Her fair hair framed her face, curling softly under her chin.

In order to reach her table, which was next to the window, Tamsin had to pass Sarne Brand's. As she followed the waiter who led her towards it, she felt Sarne Brand's watchful eyes taking in every detail of her appearance.

He was, she was certain, noting the quality of the dress, its superior cut and styling. Had it, perhaps, helped to establish her even more in his eyes as one of the idle rich? All the same, there was a certain puzzlement in his expression.

It was acute shyness—and an unexplained feeling of antagonism—which caused her to nod in his direction but without a hint of a smile. If he expected her to play the 'great lady', she would not disappoint him.

If she expected him to feel snubbed, she was disappointed. He met her greeting, not with an answering nod, but with a cool lift of the eyebrows. Colour stained her cheeks and it was she, instead, who felt disconcerted. As she stared out of the window, idly crumbling the roll on the plate, she drifted back to their tête-à-tête that afternoon.

She had met the man barely an hour before. There had

been no introduction. They hadn't even introduced themselves. Nor had she even known his name. Yet she had, without a moment's thought, cast aside the habits of a lifetime and willingly accompanied him, an almost complete stranger, to a café and accepted his hospitality.

It had been something she would not have dreamt of doing in her own country. Yet, after only an hour or two in a foreign city, she had stepped completely out of character. She wondered—and she went pink at the thought—if Sarne Brand found all the girls he had tried to pick up as easy game as she had proved to be.

The waiter placed the fruit juice she had ordered in front of her. She surfaced, turned her head and smiled her thanks at him. The smile had not faded when she caught the intense stare of her companion of the afternoon. There was a flicker in his eyes, an estimating narrowing of them as the light of her smile fell momentarily and unintentionally upon him.

Annoyed with herself, Tamsin turned back to the window. What was he thinking now? That she was giving him even more encouragement? Her first course arrived and she started on it a little absently. Why did the man have her so constantly in his line of vision? There was no need for him to have followed her that afternoon, no need for him to have bought her a coffee.

She remembered their almost silent walk back to the hotel. He had taken a shorter way, but to Tamsin it had seemed double the length of time it had taken her to reach the lake. In the entrance foyer she had thanked him for the coffee and for escorting her back. He had nodded distantly and walked away. Maybe he had grown tired of her company. Perhaps she had proved such easy prey to ensnare, she no longer presented a challenge and he had therefore lost interest.

It was with a sense of disappointment that she had climbed the stairs to her room. What had she expected, anyway? That he had singled her out, of all the women he must surely know, for special attention? And after such a short acquaintance?

Anyway, she reproached herself, he was not her type at all. In her three years of teacher-training, she had had no experience of that kind of man. Sarne Brand confused and puzzled her. She could not place him at all.

All through the meal, Tamsin was conscious of his presence. Whether or not he was equally aware of her she did not even try to discover. Her eyes, when not resting on the food she consumed, were staring at the lush foliage outside the hotel, the exotic palm trees which flourished in the humid atmosphere.

Tamsin pushed away her empty coffee cup and prepared to leave the dining-room. It was necessary before she moved to steel herself to passing Sarne Brand. Annoyingly, he remained at his table. If only she had been a little slower in eating her meal ...

She rose, glancing at him and finding with a shock that his eyes were on her. There was speculation in them as though she presented a difficult but intriguing puzzle.

As she passed his table, she tried to disguise her nervousness with a proud lift of the head. What she did not expect was a swift change of expression to a cynical, smiling lift of the eyebrows. What could his thoughts have been to have given rise to such a smile? The quick colour came again, but Tamsin was glad he did not see it because by then she had passed him.

She stood for some time on the balcony of her room. The view was hazy now and the sky clouded over. The lake was still visible, but the surrounding mountains mere outlines in the mist. There was a chill in the air which made her shiver, so she went inside to find the cashmere stole her uncle had insisted that she should add—as a gift from him —to her collection of holiday clothes.

It was curiosity which drove Tamsin to seek the hotel

lounge, curiosity and a touch of loneliness. There were armchairs in the lounge. It was extensive and opened out on to the main entrance which led to the swimming pool. Tamsin wandered towards the glass entrance doors and stood looking through them.

The swimming pool was no longer blue. It had lost its colour as darkness had descended. The water was illuminated from beneath the surface, the floodlights being sunk into the walls of the pool. The tables and chairs around it were empty, the pool deserted and tranquil.

She turned and sought a place to sit. In this luxurious building, in such exotic surroundings, she was out of her depth. The deep armchair in a corner within reach of a bookcase gave her privacy and a chance to observe others. She saw families gathered in a circle round a table on which used coffee cups stood. She saw couples conscious only of each other; older husbands and wives reading books and magazines. There was no doubt about it, she was the odd one out.

If only, she thought, she had accepted her uncle's offer to provide accommodation for a friend, too. But, she had reasoned, it would have been quite unfair to expect him to foot the bill for someone else who would simply act as her companion. Now she longed for company, for a friendly face.

It gave her a shock to realise that, while observing others, she herself had been observed. Sarne Brand had taken a chair across the room and was reclining, head against the back, legs outstretched, eyes half-closed, watching her. What was going through his head? Was he trying to place her, attempting to decide from which part of the English class structure she came?

The cold, repudiating gaze she flung back at him did not cause him the embarrassment she hoped it would. It seemed, instead, to bring him to a decision. With a hammering heart, she saw him rise, thrust his hands into his trouser pockets and wander across the hotel lounge. Her fingers felt for the bookmark in the paperback on her lap, her eyes sought the words. If she dismissed the man from her mind, blanked him out, maybe he would just disappear ...

He materialised in front of her, his attitude relaxed, his mouth curved into a mocking smile. 'You look lonely, Miss Selby.' Tamsin did not answer, she didn't even look up. It seemed he continued to look down at her because he did not move away. 'Since I appear to be the only person you know in the hotel, would you like me to join you?'

Her eyes swept up to his, the strange antagonism she felt whenever she looked at him darkening the blue-grey eyes. 'Take pity on me as you did this afternoon? No, thanks.' His smile annoyed her even more. 'It could be,' she responded coldly, 'that I prefer my own company.' That, she thought, *must* make him go away.

But his skin, she reflected acidly, must be thicker than she had judged because he stayed where he was. 'It's unusual, to say the least,' he drawled, 'to find a young woman spending her holiday alone.'

It was, Tamsin realised, another attempt on his part to delve into her personal life, but she did not give him any satisfaction on that subject.

Doggedly he pursued his subtly-phrased inquiries. 'It makes you rather—vulnerable.' At her questioning glance, he supplied, 'To the—shall we say—machinations of certain types of men?'

'Such as yourself?'

The sharp question jerked back his head in laughter, then he shook it slowly. 'Where females are concerned, I'm the one who has to employ evading tactics. I never do the running.' Her eyes opened exaggeratedly wide and he laughed again. 'You don't believe me?'

'I can't really, can I? When I arrived you carried my cases, although there was really no need.'

'Politeness. Solicitude. You looked tired and there was no porter around.'

'What about this afternoon?'

'When I followed you? Purely protective on my part. You worried me. You were in a daze as if you had stepped from another world.'

'Now?' she broke in with an "answer that" smile.

'Ah, yes. Now.' He rubbed his cheek. 'Maybe I was bored, in search of a diversion.'

Tamsin glanced around and said acidly, 'No women to chase you? No female to pander to your masculine vanity?'

'You're so right.' His gaze wandered over her and she felt the stinging colour again. She wished the man would go away. He disturbed her, irritated her, worried her ...

'For some reason,' he spoke again, 'you seem to have taken a dislike to me. Not that it worries me. I find it something of a challenge, stimulating after the constant and slightly sickening adulation which so often comes my way from so many of your sex.'

"Sickening adulation"? That he certainly would not get from her! 'Dislike you?' she murmured, simulating surprise. 'To be honest,' she went on as coolly as she could manage—it was not easy because she was about to tell a lie—'I feel absolutely nothing where you're concerned.' She watched his eyebrows lift. 'I hardly know you, anyway.' She spoke with commendable offhandedness in view of the way her heart was beating. 'A few hours——'

He shook his head in mocking disbelief. 'It seems like years.' With which inscrutable statement he went away.

But not for long. He returned a little later holding two or three newspapers. One of them he opened out and proceeded to read, having seated himself in an armchair next to Tamsin's. His choice of seat both surprised and, for some reason, irritated her. Every time the man came near she felt her skin prickle, as though he presented some imagined danger, like a ghost story told in semi-darkness.

She stole a glance at the paper in which he seemed so engrossed—but she could not read a word of it! It was a German newspaper, yet he read it as if German was his native language. There were two other newspapers on the arm of his chair and Tamsin did her best to look at them without attracting his attention. One of them was clearly Italian and the other an English one which she easily recognised.

Just before she straightened, resuming her former position, she caught him watching her over the top of the newspaper he was reading. With a mocking smile he offered her the German newspaper. She shook her head, blushing at being caught prying. His eyebrows lifted, saying a silent "No?" At which he grinned and picked up the Italian paper, proffering that.

'You know I can only speak English,' she said bad-temperedly. 'I'm not multi-lingual, as you seem to be.' She returned to her book and he to his reading. After a few moments she ventured, 'How—how many languages can you speak, Mr Brand?'

'What?' He had been so deeply engrossed in the paper the interruption had plainly irritated him.

His frown, after his good-humoured by-play of a few moments before, took her by surprise. It seemed that he did not regard his proximity to her as any reason for conversing. It had been she, Tamsin supposed ruefully, who had invaded his privacy and had wrongly assumed that, in sitting beside her, he had sought to establish communications.

'It doesn't matter,' she said tautly, wishing she could rewind her question like tape in a cassette recorder.

But he must have heard what she had said because he answered shortly, 'Eight. Or it may be nine. I forget.' With that, he dismissed the subject and she did not dare to question him further although she longed to do so.

She snapped her book shut and rose. Immediately, he

lowered the newspaper and asked, 'What are you doing?'

'Removing my irritating presence.' She made for the entrance doors which led to the drive and next to it, the deserted, floodlit swimming pool. But she did not go outside. Instead she stood at the top of the steps and gazed around, seeing the gaily coloured lights strung from tree to tree and the empty tables and chairs around the pool.

Someone came to stand beside her. 'Where are you going?'

The autocratic attitude which the man adopted towards her irritated her beyond words. Her head turned and she looked up into his face. It was in shadow, whereas hers caught the full glare of the floodlights which illuminated the hotel walls.

'I'm over age, Mr Brand. I'm considered in law as being responsible for my own actions.'

A flare of anger burnt behind his eyes, only to be extinguished moments later by a crusting of frost. He was clearly a man used to deference from those around him and resented being spoken to with such audacity.

'The *law* may consider you responsible, Miss Selby,' he said curtly, 'but I don't.' Tamsin felt the grip of a punishing hand. 'It was this arm, wasn't it, that I caught in order to pull you back from going under the wheels of a car?'

She winced and tried to free herself. His touch hurt, humiliated—and disturbed her immoderately.

'Please let me go.' Her voice was controlled. She had succeeded in keeping the pain she was experiencing at his hands out of it.

'If I do, will you dash out into the night—maybe get lost in the big city, or worse, molested?' He was smiling again. How quickly his moods changed! His hold had slackened, but his hand lingered, softly now, just a little caressing, as if he enjoyed the feel of her ...

Of course he did, she admonished herself. He would enjoy the feel of any woman.

Tamsin shivered, pretending that the cool air of evening had chilled her skin. Even to herself she would not admit that the man troubled her, stirring into life feelings which, until now, despite the fact that she had lived twenty-two years of her life, had lain slumbering unworriedly like a babe in arms.

'I assure you, I'm not going out. I'm tired. I've had a long day of travelling, so *please*, Mr Brand——' Large grey-blue eyes, flecked by pinpoints of multicoloured lights whose reflection they caught, sought his.

He gazed into the upturned eyes and murmured in Italian, words that brought a smile to his mouth. Then he spoke in English, but what he said was as incomprehensible to Tamsin as the foreign language he had just used.

'A long day,' he said, 'months, years ... I think,' he went on softly, 'I'm going to enjoy Miss Tamsin Selby's visit to Lugano.'

He let her go at last. '*Buona notte, signorina*,' he murmured. 'Sleep well. We shall meet again.'

Tamsin, reaching her room, leant back against the door. She closed her eyes, trying to shut out the handsome face, the sardonic smile. But in the darkness behind her eyelids the face stood out more clearly—mocking, cynical, remote —or, when the mood took him, charming enough to break any vulnerable young woman's heart.

CHAPTER THREE

THE morning was blue and golden, with a promising veil of mist over the distant mountains. Tamsin showered and pulled on her sundress. She combed her wayward hair, then sighed with the sheer delight of experiencing, if only for a few brief weeks, the luxury that surrounded her.

She stepped on to the balcony that overlooked the swimming pool. Already there were a handful of people swimming and splashing. Some time that day, she promised herself, she would put on her swimsuit and join the crowds down there.

Breakfast was self-service and taken on the terrace. Hesitating a moment before pouring herself a glass of orange juice, Tamsin looked around her like a creature of the wild making sure that no enemy was watching, circling, awaiting her weakest moment to pounce...

Her enemy was missing. She sighed with relief and filled a glass with fruit juice. In her other hand she carried a plate of rolls, crisp bread and cheeses. Later, she would return for the coffee.

She was nearly through the meal when Sarne Brand walked through the doors and on to the terrace. Like her, he glanced round, not with nervousness as she had done but with a kind of anticipation. Neither was he searching for an enemy. To Tamsin, who saw the keen, alert look in his eyes, the predator was seeking unprotected, inattentive quarry. When his watchful eyes alighted on her, Tamsin shrank into herself and felt the urge to race for cover.

He smiled, raising a lazy hand in her direction. She gave a quick, nervous nod and concentrated on her breakfast. She felt him approach and held her breath. She cursed the fact that there was an empty chair opposite her. When he passed by, his hands full as hers had been, and he did not even pause to exchange a word, she felt incredibly disappointed.

He found a seat two tables from hers with a young couple who called his name and invited him to join them. It seemed he was popular because other people called, '*Guten morgen*, Herr Brand,' and '*Bonjour*, Monsieur Brand.' And she had not even said 'Good morning'!

All around her there was laughter and chatter—and she could not understand a word. If only, she reproached herself, she had learnt just a little German, a few phrases of

Italian ... Families came out on to the sun-dappled terrace. Groups of friends gathered round tables pushed together. She, it seemed, was the only guest who ate alone.

Tamsin collected her coffee and sipped it slowly, giving it time to cool. She wondered, a little forlornly, if she would enjoy this holiday as much as she had anticipated. What she had not realised was, luxury or no luxury, how lonely it was possible to feel amongst a crowd.

She sighed, thinking, This is a never-to-be-repeated holiday. I must make the most of it.

'So sad?' It was a voice that made her heart jump and sent an electric shock through her system. 'May I?' Without waiting for her answer, Sarne Brand pulled out the empty chair and sat opposite her with his coffee.

She was annoyed with the colour that washed over her cheeks, with the way her pulses leapt and the way her whole being was suffused with a new life. She was annoyed with all these things yet she smiled. She smiled, she told herself reassuringly, because for a few minutes, for as long as it would take Sarne Brand to drink his coffee, she would not be sitting alone.

He smiled back and the world spun like a top. When it returned to its normal stability, the smile was still curving the full mouth, displacing completely the cynicism which Tamsin had come to expect.

'Any plans for today?' he asked, eyeing her over the rim of his cup. He seemed to find her smooth, sloping shoulders of immense interest. His scrutiny made Tamsin wish she had pulled on a jacket over her sundress before coming down to breakfast. 'A seat in the sun, judging by your outfit.'

She nodded. 'A swim first. The pool looks so inviting I can't resist it.'

'Don't even try. It's delightful. I've been in it many times.'

Now was her chance and she took it. 'Do—do you live here, in this hotel?'

The faintest pause, the slightest narrowing of his eyes, then, 'I am at the moment, yes.'

'So——' she tried to make a joke of it to hide her inquisitiveness, 'so we're both members of the—the privileged classes. Neither of us needs——' if she went on she would be acting a lie, but she continued nevertheless, 'needs to earn our living?'

He was too astute to be caught by her cleverly-phrased question. He smiled, but there was no amusement behind it. It was plain he resented her seemingly clumsy manner of prying into his private life. 'You think my life is one long holiday?'

She did not take warning from the edge to his voice. 'Your wife, she——' Tamsin paused, waiting for the denial of the existence of such a person. None came and she swallowed hard. Having started she had to go on. She was becoming more and more involved with her own verbal machinations. 'She——' What could she say? 'Are you ... I thought maybe you were—well, parted from her?'

He smiled down at the tablecloth. Then he looked up quickly. 'Your husband—doesn't he object to your coming all this way on your own, a perfect prey for the masculine predators, the men who prowl the world looking for such innocents abroad as you?'

'I haven't *got* a husband,' she almost cried. 'I'm not even engaged.'

His grin stopped her. 'Thanks for telling me. That's all I wanted to know.'

He had been so much more clever than she had been! He had discovered that she was single, apparently heart-whole—and told her in a roundabout way that he regarded her as unworldly, ingenuous and quite unable to take care of herself.

Annoyed that he now knew all about her marital status, yet she was as ignorant as before about his, she responded with rancour, 'So in your opinion I ought to have someone to hold my hand everywhere I go in the daytime and a teddy bear to cuddle at night!'

His grin broadened and his eyes made a lazy tour of her body from the top of her head over her shoulders, dwelling on the swelling shape beneath the sundress and moving down as far as the table would allow. 'Most certainly, Miss Selby. You definitely need your hand held during the day. But during the night?' The lazy eyes narrowed, holding hers. 'I can think of better things for a girl to hold in her arms than a teddy bear!'

He looked on her deepening colour with amusement. He rose, pushing in his chair. 'If you'll excuse me ...'

Disappointment forced a question from her and she regretted it at once. 'Will you—will you be in to lunch?'

He waited a moment, then, 'I'm not sure. Why, do you want me to be?'

Tamsin was appalled with herself for letting him know how she was coming to rely on his company, to expect it as her due and more, to enjoy it. She forced her shoulders to shrug and her head to shake unconcernedly.

Sarne smiled an inscrutable kind of smile which made her want to pinch herself with annoyance. To a man with his looks, and his enigmatic charm, after whom women must surely chase in their dozens—whether or not he was married —a question such as she had asked him, in the anxious tone she had unwittingly used, must be as good as an intimation that her favours were his for the asking.

'*Addio, signorina.*' He gave a mocking bow. 'Enjoy your swim.'

Tamsin did indeed enjoy her swim. She plunged in, swam for a while, climbed out and towelled herself lightly. Then she sat in a chair at the water's edge, her scarlet bikini brilliant in the morning sun. A middle-aged couple joined her, the woman in a sundress, her husband in shorts and short-sleeved shirt.

It seemed that they were Dutch, but their English was so good Tamsin found herself conversing with them with ease. Yes, she was from England, she told them, and yes, she was on holiday in Switzerland for the first time. Did she mind being alone? they asked. They had noticed her at her table ...

'You have no friend,' the husband said, smiling, 'no— how do the English say—young man?'

'Oh,' Tamsin laughed, 'boy-friends. One or two, maybe, but only friends, nothing serious.' She had a career, she told them—at least, she *thought* she had a career, but——

'Why, Mr Brand,' the wife said, glancing over her shoulder, 'have you come to sunbathe with us? Find a chair ——' But Sarne remained standing beside them.

How long, Tamsin thought angrily, had Sarne Brand been there? Had he been listening to the conversation? Sarne addressed the Dutch couple in their own language and Tamsin wondered again how many languages he could speak. Where had he learnt them, and what did he do with his knowledge of them? Waste it, she thought spitefully, in the idle life he led, living as a permanent resident in a luxury hotel?

She rose, then immediately wished she had remained seated. Sarne's eyes swung to look at her. Her cheeks burned at his expression which was part admiration and part taunting.

'My dear young lady,' the husband of the Dutch woman said, 'we are so sorry to speak in our native tongue when you are present. Please forgive us——'

Tamsin smiled. 'I don't mind at all.' She gave Sarne Brand a swift provocative look. 'I only wish I were as clever as Mr Brand and spoke your language—plus a dozen others, of course. When you're with him, it's like being accompanied by a language laboratory on two legs.' She took no heed of his tightening lips. 'I'm sure that somewhere on him there's a button you can press and wind him back to start the lesson all over again.'

The Dutch couple laughed, enjoying the joke. Sarne Brand's smile did not alter, but his eyes cooled visibly. 'Just try "pressing" me, Miss Selby, and see what kind of lesson you learn. Especially,' his eyes sauntered over her, 'dressed as you are now.'

The quick colour came again and she turned to her two companions. 'Please excuse me.' Sarne Brand she ignored. She made for the swimming pool steps, descended them backwards and dropped down to float lazily in the sunshine. After a while she turned over and swam, arm over arm from one end of the pool to the other. When she stopped for breath she trod water, grasping the bar around the edge. She looked for the Dutch couple, certain that by now Sarne would have left them.

They had gone, but Sarne remained and he made no attempt to hide the fact that, of all the people in that pool, she was the one who interested him the most. If only, she thought, the colour of her swimsuit was not so brilliant. Then he would not be able to pick her out so easily.

As she looked at him he smiled sardonically as if thinking to himself, Another conquest. See how she's looking for me. Angry with herself, she pushed with her feet against the side and glided through the water. Moments later, her head came up of its own accord and she found her eyes seeking for him yet again. Yes, he was still there and his attention had not wandered. Was he counting the number of times she sought him out?

His hand lifted in a salute and he turned away. Where was he going? Tamsin wondered, panicking. If he went out, she would be alone again ... Before she could stop herself, she was clambering up the steps and out of the pool. Her bare feet made damp marks on the concrete and even when they hit the hot tarmac of the entrance drive she did not flinch. She had to know where he was going!

She came to a halt as he got into a large car with a Swiss registration number. As he started the engine and began slowly to manoeuvre the car out of the parking place, Tamsin moved from behind a bush. She started walking slowly after the car, a forlorn, dripping figure barely covered by two brief pieces of scarlet. Sarne was staring ahead so she did not have to worry about his seeing her.

But she had forgotten the driving mirror in which her slight but shapely figure must have shown up like a traffic light at 'Stop'—red for danger. The driver braked, the door came open and Sarne Brand's head and shoulders twisted towards her.

'What are you doing?' he called, 'following me to my destination like a pet dog following its beloved master? Can't you bear me out of your sight?'

It was, of course, revenge for the remarks she had made about him in front of the Dutch guests. With cheeks the colour of her bikini, she turned and ran, leaping into the pool and causing a splash which made other people shriek with surprise and laughter.

Sarne was in for lunch. Tamsin, who was already at her table, saw him come into the dining-room. Her heart hammered and she kept her eyes riveted on the lush greenery beyond the windows, pretending she had not seen him. She tensed, convinced that he would come to her table before going to his, if only to follow up the advantage his verbal victory had given him over her that morning.

He did no such thing. He seated himself at his table and picked up the menu, pretending that *she* was not there! Piqued, Tamsin tore at the roll beside her, pushing pieces into her mouth until she almost choked. It was her pride he had hurt, both now and earlier, she told herself. She would have liked to have torn *him* into pieces as she had torn her roll.

The meal was delicious, but she hurried through it, so as to remove herself from the dining-room with all possible speed. She didn't want to give him the chance of lingering at her table on his way out, making sarcastic conversation. But she did not escape him entirely. Without bothering to fold her table napkin, she pushed it aside and stood up. If only she did not have to pass his table!

As she drew level with it, he glanced up and met her eyes. She noticed with surprise that during his meal he had been reading through a pile of closely-typewritten papers. He smiled. 'You see, I came back for lunch.'

'Did you?' She did her best to sound offhand. 'I didn't notice.'

'Liar,' he commented, and continued with his reading.

Once again he had got the better of her and, moreover, dismissed her like a teacher sending away a pestering schoolchild. Her head was high as she left the dining-room, but humiliation trailed her like a second shadow.

In her room she lingered on the balcony, her eyes scanning the view but her thoughts wandering back to the dark, bent head she had left behind in the dining-room. What had been so absorbing to him in those papers he had been studying? Was the man, perhaps, a businessman working overseas for his company? Or was he simply a man who was so wealthy he had no need to work, and could afford to spend his days whiling away the time as a hotel guest? In other words, an absolutely useless member of society?

The last idea pleased her most, fitting in with her desire to hit back at him for the way he kept winning their strange little skirmishes. The man was an enigma and she would waste no more time thinking about him.

There was a knock on her door, decisive and demanding admittance. She could hear it clearly from the balcony. When she opened it, she saw Sarne Brand. It took her a second or two to recover from her surprise. Why *did* her pulse rate speed up whenever he came into view? She was so confused, she just stood and looked at him. What should she do?

He resolved the problem by taking a step inside. 'Thanks for inviting me in,' he said, smiling blandly.

'I didn't,' she replied, 'but you look as if you're the kind of man who's used to walking, with or without permission, into ladies' hotel bedrooms.'

His smile cooled. 'It seems you've placed me in the "playboy" category.' He strolled to the window. 'On what evidence, I wonder?'

Tamsin searched in her mind for a reason. 'On your—your whole attitude to life——'

He did not turn. 'What do you know about my attitude to life? We met barely twenty-four hours ago.'

'I placed you the moment I saw you,' she said defensively, feeling that once again he was about to get the better of her. 'The moment I heard you speak, I thought——'

He swung round, his eyes open wide. 'The moment you saw me? Heard me speak? The arrogance! Not to say impudence! And from a girl who, although without a job, can afford to live for one month—or was it two?—in a luxury hotel in a part of the world which is not exactly renowned for its cheapness.' Why, she wondered, was he so angry? 'And from a girl,' he went on, 'who, because she's feeling so lonely amongst a crowd, has fastened on to me like a shipwrecked sailor to an upturned boat? And who, every time I come into view, looks up hopefully, willing me to come and sit with her? Yes, big eyes, I've noticed it all. I'm neither blind nor unintelligent.'

Her cheeks burned at the truths he was flinging at her.

'What am I supposed to take you for—a lonely little innocent in a big, bad world? Or,' his eyes half closed, 'should it be playgirl to my playboy?' He walked towards her, hands in pockets. 'You wouldn't be after me, would you? You wouldn't be giving me the old green light—green for "go"—or, in this case, "come"?'

He stood directly in front of her, so close she could feel his breath. 'Because if so, there's no time like the present, as they say. And no place like a luxurious bedroom—and no doubt equally luxurious bed. I'm entirely male and, with a girl with your attractions, more than willing.'

She backed away, frightened now, her body throbbing with humiliation and, she could not deny it, an impermissible excitement.

'Seduction scenes have taken place on much shorter acquaintances than ours,' he persisted, 'so don't let a mere twenty-four hours' knowledge of each other worry you.' He followed as she retreated—and came up against the bed. She stood rigidly against it, determined to remain upright and not to fall back on to it, however near he came.

His hands rested on her waist. Warmth crept into his eyes, a softness into his smile. 'Shall we improve our acquaintance, Miss Selby? You haven't screamed like an outraged virgin. You haven't said a word to stop me. So you can't blame me if I interpret your lack of opposition as an invitation.' He moved closer and she felt him against her.

Panic constricted her throat, almost suffocating her. She had had no experience of such a situation. She was paralysed with fear, with doubt—and with a frightening fascination.

His hands about her waist exerted greater pressure, pulling her against him. 'Well,' he said softly, 'is it yes or no?'

The hard feel of him, the male-type scent of his lotion, the melting, mesmerising look in his brown eyes roused her senses until she wanted to cry out, 'yes, yes!'

Then it was as if she were in an aircraft looking down at the scene below, at herself, her principles, at her very beliefs and ideals. Every detail showed up, every fault in her behaviour where he was concerned since she had arrived. Every word he had said about her was true. But she would not lower her standards for any man.

'Please,' her voice was tremulous yet firm, 'take away your hands. Let me go. This isn't——' She felt his breath on her face again. 'This isn't my way at all.'

Slowly the pressure on her waist eased and she was free to move whenever she wished. She hoped he did not notice the merest hesitation that came before she broke all contact with his person.

It was impossible to meet his eyes. If that was what he thought of her—that she was a wealthy young woman in search of a man, any man—wasn't she, after all, there alone, and hadn't she told him she had no job?—then the sooner their acquaintance came to an end the better.

Tamsin went to the window and gazed out of it. 'I'm sorry,' she said, so quietly she could hardly hear herself speak, 'if I've made a nuisance of myself. I'm sorry if I've led you on,' bitterly, 'raised your hopes only to dash them. I'm sorry if I've looked at you too much. And'—she had to swallow her pride—'and for misjudging you. Not to mention,' a whisper now, 'being impudent to you.'

Footsteps approached and she tensed. If only the man did not have such an effect on her reflexes! Then he was behind her. 'Have you finished abasing yourself, Miss Selby?' He spoke softly and as if he were smiling. 'It seems I, too, owe you an apology—for misjudging you.'

She shook her head. 'It doesn't matter.' Then, because she felt she should try to explain, she said, 'If I—if I have—well, as you said, "fastened" on to you——'

'Forget it,' he said abruptly.

Tamsin half-turned. 'No, it's true. I did, in a sense, come to rely on you, but only'—she was telling this stranger too much about herself—'only because I'm rather shy.' She turned away, back to the window. 'It was you who helped me when I arrived. Yours was the only face I knew. You—you were a kind of lifeline.'

There was a long pause and she waited to hear his footsteps taking him from the room. When a man had been thwarted by a woman, as he had been, who could blame him for walking away?

Tamsin tensed as his hands came to rest on her shoulders. 'Miss Selby?'

'Yes, Mr Brand?'

'Shall we start all over again? Shall we pretend that everything that's happened in the past twenty-four hours was fiction and not fact, and that we've just met?'

'If you like, Mr Brand,' she whispered.

'My name is Sarne. Will you call me that, if I call you Tamsin?' She nodded. 'Good. Give me your hand.' He turned her gently. 'We'll shake on it.'

But he did not shake her hand, he held it, studying its shape. His eyes lifted suddenly to hers and she saw in his large brown eyes, his high-boned cheeks and his well-shaped, full lips the part of him that he must have inherited from his Italian–Swiss mother.

No Englishman this, with those black arched brows, those long eyelashes, that thick, dark hair. The white teeth, the caressing look, the winning smile—they all added up to a seductive Latin charm which made her heart turn over. She pulled herself up. What was the matter with her? This man was not only a stranger, he was practised in the art of attracting women. He was not her kind at all.

Carefully, trying not to offend, she withdrew her hand from his. 'I'm glad we're still going to be *friends*,' she said firmly.

'Friends.' He considered the expression. 'A good word. Yes,' he looked her over, 'I shall enjoy being your *friend*.' His emphasis held implications hers had not. 'I have to go visiting this afternoon,' Sarne remarked. 'What will you do, Tamsin?'

Hearing him speak her name made her heart skip. It sounded different, sweeter and with a strange significance ... So he was going out again. She must not let him see her

42

disappointment. His sarcasm might return, he might accuse her once more of clinging.

'I don't know what I'll do,' she answered. 'Go looking for the shops, perhaps.'

'Good. Have you enough Swiss money, travellers' cheques?'

'I've got plenty of money,' she told him brightly. 'I'm loaded with Swiss francs. My——' She stopped. My uncle gave me handfuls, she had been going to say. But her uncle's name was forbidden to pass her lips.

'Your——?' The faintest narrowing of those brown eyes had the colour creeping into her cheeks. He was thinking badly of her again, but she could not enlighten him. His suspicions would have to remain uncorrected.

He did not press her for an answer. He went to the door. 'Maybe I shall see you again this evening. Good shopping.' He lifted his hand and was gone.

So casual a leave-taking when only a few minutes before he had been all set to make passionate love to her! How little it would have meant to him if she had allowed him to do so. And how much, a small but worrying voice whispered, it would have meant to her.

Tamsin caught a trolleybus to the shops. It took her along the busy main road which ran by the lakeside—the road from which, the day before, an angry hand had reached out and grasped her, pulling her back from the brink of disaster.

Dazzled by the goods on display, catching her breath at the price of them, admiring the beauty of the diamond-studded watches and jewellery, she wandered through the shopping areas and under the ancient arcades.

She did not have the courage to sit at a table at one of the many pavement cafés. Yet she longed for a drink to moisten her dry throat and take a rest from walking in the intense heat. If only Sarne were with her, he—— She checked her foolish thoughts. There she was again, using him, even in her imagination, as a prop on which to lean.

It was a beautiful evening. After dinner Tamsin sat for a while in the hotel lounge. She had delayed dining, hoping that by the time she went to the dining-room, Sarne would have returned. Even if he sat in his usual isolation at his table for one, she would at least have a glimpse of him— maybe, if their truce still held, he would smile and acknowledge her presence, if nothing else!

But he had not come. Disappointed, she had gone up to her room and gazed at the mountains, perhaps even more beautiful in the evening sun. Then, feeling lonely again, she had gone downstairs and exchanged a few words with the Dutch guests who were drinking their coffee at a low table.

Tamsin searched among the newspapers for an English one, found the previous day's edition and took it to an armchair to read. It was not that she was especially anxious for news of home. All the troubles and tribulations of her homeland seemed far away at that moment, even the fact that when she did return, there would not be a job for her to go back to.

It was, rather, that a newspaper gave her such an expanse behind which to hide, and over which she could peep now and then at the passing guests. That way she would see Sarne Brand without his seeing her looking for him!

But she had no need to see him in order to know he was there. She heard his voice—she was even becoming sensitive to that now—and although he spoke to the Dutch guests in their own language, she recognised the voice as his nonetheless. Someone hailed him from across the lounge and he replied in French. Some German people greeted him and he answered in their language, too.

Tamsin, open-eyed, lowered the newspaper a fraction. What was he, this man Sarne Brand? A verbal chameleon, changing not his colour but his speech to suit the circumstances? His back was turned to her, so she could safely gaze her fill while he conversed in fluent—and presumably perfect—German. His slacks were dark blue and well-fitting, his matching casual jacket belted and unbuttoned. The black hair was well-groomed and touched the jacket collar, while one hand was pushed into a pocket.

If only he would turn round, Tamsin thought, but hastily lifted the newspaper high in case he did so. She heard him say, '*Auf Wiedersehen,*' which she assumed meant 'goodbye', because after that there were footsteps moving in the direction of the dining-room. She willed her hands to remain steady as they held the newspaper.

A hand fastened on to the top of the pages and a face appeared over the top. '*Bonjour,* Mademoiselle Selby. *Parlez-vous français?*'

Sarne Brand laughed down at her and she lowered the newspaper to her lap. She saw that his tie was blue, matching his jacket and his shirt a startling white. He had dressed for dinner with careful informality. Her heart began its habitual dance as indeed it did whenever he was in the vicinity and she smiled up at him.

'*Un peu, monsieur. Mais,*' she paused, doing her best to recall her school French, '*je comprends mieux l'anglais.*'

He laughed loudly. '*Très bien, mademoiselle.* We'll make a linguist of you yet!'

'How did you know it was me, Sarne?'

He tutted. 'Grammar! Learn to speak your own language correctly, first. "I" not "me". How did I know it was you?' He looked down. 'Your delectable legs.' She blushed at the sudden familiarity. 'The way you were hiding from me so frantically.' Hiding from him? she thought. If only he knew the truth! 'Not to mention,' he went on, 'something you might call—instinct.'

There was an awkward pause as she felt his eyes upon

her. 'Have you—have you dined, Sarne?'

'No. Have you?' She nodded. 'When I've eaten, may I join you?'

She frowned. 'You join *me*?'

His eyebrows lifted. 'I don't see why not. Unless you'd rather I——'

'Of course you can join me, Sarne,' she broke in hastily, the colour giving away her pleasure. 'I—I should only be alone otherwise.'

'Yes,' a little dryly, 'that's what I thought.' And with that enigmatic statement he said, '*Au revoir*,' and disappeared into the dining-room.

By the time he reappeared, Tamsin had reached such a state of agitation it frightened her. How could she have allowed herself to become so involved with a man she had met only the day before? She told herself yet again it was because he was English—well, half English—that he was good company, easy to talk to and, moreover, had taken pity on her because of her solitariness.

If he had made approaches to her, suggesting a closer relationship, could she blame him? Wouldn't any man have done so, given the encouragement she had undoubtedly given him? That he was male in every sense of the word, she had no doubt. She was more aware of him than she had been of any other man she had met.

He was also more mature, more sure of himself, with a greater knowledge of the ways of the world—and, there was no doubt about it, of women. The young men with whom she had worked at the college of education had been far less self-assured, younger in their ways and outlook, and of course, her own age. Sarne Brand, she calculated, must be ten years older than she was.

He approached, running a hand over his hair. 'A walk is indicated, I think. I'm eating far too much in this place. If I don't watch out, I shall begin to develop a middle-aged bulge.' He patted his waistline.

'You,' she said, rising, 'middle-aged? You're far too young——'

He gave a low bow. '*Grazie, signorina*. I'm thirty-four. To you, no doubt—how old are you, twenty?'

'Add two.'

'Twenty-two. No doubt to you I'm nearing my dotage.' Tamsin gave a vehement shake of the head, but he said, 'It's time we went—that is, if you'd like to come for a walk?'

She would love to, she said, and made to go towards the doors, but Sarne's hand caught her arm. 'It's a fine evening, but it may be cooler than it looks. Haven't you a jacket of some kind upstairs?'

Her dress was sleeveless with a deceptively simple cut. It had not been cheap, having been paid for with her uncle's money. His warnings about the wealth of the other guests and his desire that she should not look like a Cinderella among them had overridden her reluctance to spend money which did not belong to her.

The dress had a jacket to match, but she shook her head. 'It's all right. I won't get cold, I'm sure. I——'

He smiled. 'Go and get it, please.' She heard it again, that faint ring of authority. Now and then it made itself apparent, at the most unexpected moments, and when it did, it would brook no arguments.

Still she hesitated, however. Would he have changed his mind by the time she returned from getting the jacket? She frowned. If he did, it would mean another evening spent alone ...

'Don't worry. I won't run away.' Could the man read her thoughts? 'But don't be long. You've quite enough make-up on your face. Your hair looks fine, there's nothing at all wrong with you. So there's no need to linger in front of the mirror.' He glanced at his watch. 'I'll give you three minutes. If you're any longer, I'll come and get you. And,' with a glint, 'you know what could happen if I made my way into your bedroom again!'

It was threat enough and she was off, hearing his laughter.

The sky, a fading blue turning to gold as the sun set behind the darkening mountains, was telling of the coming of night. The shops were closed, although the cafés stayed open, but the noise, the excited chatter of the tourists had hardly changed.

Sarne pulled Tamsin's arm through his and led her through the underpass and up the steps to the lakeside. They walked to the jetty where the lake steamers arrived and departed. The boats were painted white and red and the Swiss flag flew in the breeze. Above the superstructure was the upper deck with its canvas awning acting as a shelter from rain or sun. Even at that time of day the boats were operating, unloading passengers and taking them on board.

There were shops and kiosks selling souvenirs and postcards. Round the bay and to the right stood another mountain, tapering towards the summit.

'San Salvatore,' Sarne said. 'Some time I'll take you up there. There's a funicular railway to the top.'

Some time, Tamsin thought. Would that 'some time' ever come? Men and their promises—they never kept them, especially one as sought-after by women as this man must be.

They did not linger but walked along the promenade, alongside the trees which had been pollarded to ensure that they all grew to the same height. Along the lake and in the distance the line of mountains showed darkly, the golden-yellow of the sunglow revealing a haziness which promised well for the next day.

Sarne sighed, feeling for Tamsin's hand and grasping it. 'It's a long time since I did this.' She looked up at him inquiringly, hoping the dusk would hide from him her excitement at his touch. 'Walk along the lake, I mean, in the cool of the evening, bemused and curious, like a tourist.'

'So you're—not a tourist?' She ventured the question, tensing for the rebuke she thought must come.

He laughed softly and considered the question. 'Not really, no.' If Tamsin had expected any more information, she did not get it.

'Did you mean——' Should she ask, would he regard the question as 'impertinent'? 'Did you mean with a woman?'

She felt him stiffen, but he must have overcome his annoyance because he laughed. 'Still trying to discover whether I have a love life?'

'Well,' she hoped he would not see her blush, 'you—you are walking with me like—like this.' She indicated their linked hands.

'So you consider that *you* may be my love life?' That seemed to amuse him even more. 'Are you expecting me to propose at the end of the evening? Come, come, this is the twentieth century. Things don't happen that way any more.'

She coloured again, this time with anger. She did not know why she was so angry, but she tried to disengage her hand from his. 'Don't be silly! That isn't what I meant at all.'

He stilled with ease her struggles to free herself and retained her hand in his. 'All right, *cara*,' he said softly. 'Calm yourself.'

'Anyway,' she responded defensively, 'you don't know anything about *my* private life.'

'Have you got one?' He spoke with mock innocence. 'I thought you told me you were unattached?'

'I said I wasn't engaged, but that didn't mean I—I— well, I hadn't got a—a boy-friend.'

'Have you?' he looked down at her.

'Well, I'—she prevaricated—'two or three. Not a special one.'

He threw back his head, laughing. 'So you go in for quantity rather than quality?' She turned to him furiously and he bent swiftly and brushed her upturned lips with his. 'That leaves the field wide open for a man like me, doesn't it?'

She frowned. 'What do you mean, a man like you? Do you consider yourself "quality"?'

He smiled. 'Don't we all?' So he evaded the question.

He pulled her to a standstill, facing the lake. It was dark now and lights were coming on all over the town, floodlights illuminating giant hotel blocks, street lamps glowing among the avenue of trees, lights reflected in the lake, shimmering, elongated, reds and yellows and greens. A steamer, alight from stem to stern with coloured lamps and alive with people singing and dancing, swished across the water, leaving its trail behind.

Not far from the shore a group of swans passed by, white shadows on the calm water. In the distance, fountains played, rising brilliantly from out of the dark depths of the lake, spreading their spray, shooting high, curling outward, their colours changing, passing through a sequence from yellow to orange to red and green. The mountain, Monte Brè, rose into the darkness like an incandescent pyramid, having so many lights on its roads and buildings and in its houses that it looked as if it were illuminated from inside.

All around, people passed, happy in their holiday mood. Cardigans hung from shoulders, jackets were draped over arms. Tamsin pulled off her jacket and at once Sarne took it from her.

'You see what I mean?' he mocked as they moved on. 'Politeness, good manners. It goes with the quality!' His arm went round her shoulders, his hand resting on her bare flesh in a light, caressing motion.

The action aroused disturbing feelings within her, profound sensations she had never experienced before. 'Please don't.' She looked up at him. In the light that was all around them she saw his eyebrows lift. He was asking her, Why not? She ran her tongue over her lips. 'I—I told you, that's not my way. I only met you yesterday, and——'

'Time enough to know,' he responded, smiling at the ground and leaving his arm where it was.

'To—to know what?'

'For a man to know, "This is a girl I could go for".' His eyes glinted. 'Given the right encouragement, of course.'

'I don't know what you mean.' When he did not explain, she rushed on, 'Anyway, I couldn't have you as a man friend.'

'Oh? Why not?'

'We're in different leagues.'

'What is that supposed to mean?'

'We come from different worlds.'

'I doubt it. You're here, staying in a luxury hotel. Your clothes are not cheap off-the-peg affairs—yes, I know enough about women to have spotted that. You must have money behind you to have enabled you to contemplate staying in such surroundings, not as a tourist would, for a week or two, but a month—or two.'

'But I—my——' She could go no further. She could not let her uncle down. Don't tell a soul who you are, he'd said. Don't let on about your relationship to me.

'Yes?' Sarne persisted. But this time it was she who chose to be silent.

They wandered along, he looking about him half-interestedly, as though he had seen it all before, she with her head down thinking over his words.

'Are you implying,' she said at last, 'that you have "money behind you" as you say—I mean, as I have? That you've got as much money as you want, more than enough, in fact, enough to enable you to live—not just stay—in a hotel like the Tranquillité?'

He laughed, deflecting the question. 'Are you a representative of the income tax authorities in disguise?'

So he would not tell her anything about himself? 'All

right, if I am probing, it's your fault. It was you who put us in "the same worlds".'

He lifted his shoulders. '*Touché!* All right, draw your own conclusions.'

'I—I don't see where this conversation is getting us,' she said tartly.

'No?' He drew her into the shadow of the trees, pulled her firmly into his arms and gave her a lingering kiss. 'That's where it's getting us,' he whispered.

'Please,' she choked, fighting the delight his nearness and the pressure of his mouth had aroused, 'don't do that.'

'Why?' He was smiling. 'You liked it too much? In that case——'

His head came down again and the world, the warm, scented romantic world around them was blotted out for the second time. The kiss was more searching, bolder, more passionate. When he released her at last, he gazed down into her face which was illuminated by the lamps all around. She did not try to pull away this time but stayed in his arms, pressed against him.

In the semi-darkness she saw the outline of his features, the classically straight nose, the full lips, the enigmatic eyes. The warm-blooded Italian inheritance was there in his face, in the closeness of his embrace, in the speed with which he had cast aside all the barriers erected by the briefness of their acquaintance which an Englishman would take days to negotiate and overcome.

'I should like,' he whispered, feathering her lips, 'to have a love affair with you.'

It was as well, she thought, that he couldn't see the wild antics of her heart. 'Lasting a month,' she said, attempting to inject some bitterness into her voice but only succeeding in sounding breathless.

'Or two,' he added, smiling.

She shook her head. 'It's not——'

'My way,' he finished. 'As you've said before. But what's

this'—he held her away, looking down at her, then pulling her back—'if it's not your way? You're in my arms, accepting my kisses. I haven't noticed any attempt on your part to build a wall between us and put me on the other side. And don't tell me,' he bent his head and moved his lips against her ear, 'it's just because you're lonely, because I simply wouldn't swallow that.'

Her cheek found his chest, resting against the white shirt under his open jacket. 'Sarne, please ...'

'All right,' he laughed indulgently, 'we'll make haste slowly, as they say. We'll go at a pace which is more suitable for a well-brought-up English girl.'

'Now you're being sarcastic.'

'Am I?' with mock surprise. 'I thought I was being truthful.' They moved out of the shelter of the trees and walked on, arms round each other, like two people deeply in love.

It's not possible, Tamsin thought. I couldn't have met this man only yesterday! I haven't fallen for him heart and soul, forsaking all others ... She drew herself up—the wedding ceremony! Her subconscious mind was playing tricks. Marriage was one thing this man would not offer, even if he were free——

'Sarne? Are you married?'

'Married?' There was a quizzical lift of his eyebrow. 'Do I detect the sound of wedding bells in your ears?' Annoyed now, she dropped her arm from his waist and tried to pull away. He pulled her back, holding her arm firmly in place against his hip. 'No, I'm not married. Would I be behaving like this with you if I were?'

'You might,' in a small voice. 'There's a sort of man-code, isn't there, that permits a male, whether tied legally to a woman or not, to take what he wants from any woman—provided she's willing to give it—without too much condemnation from society? It seems to have been so from the beginning of mankind,' now the bitterness was real, 'up to the present day. From royalty and heads of governments downwards, it doesn't seem to matter what their status. How a man behaves in his work or his vocation is one thing. How he behaves with women is judged separately—and indulgently—by the rest of his fellow men. But if you're a woman and break the moral code imposed on her——'

'Say no more, sweet Tamsin. You've made your point. Unfortunately, it's true, and there seems to be nothing one can do about it.'

'Well, I for one won't be party to it.'

He smiled down at her. 'I'll remember that.'

Tamsin heard the resolution in his voice and she knew he would.

They re-entered the hotel hand in hand. The Dutch couple greeted them, noting their linked hands and smiling. Tamsin hoped her happiness did not show. When Sarne asked if she would like a drink, she accepted gladly, not because she wanted the drink but because the dimmer lighting of the bar would be kinder to her flushed cheeks.

There were low modern chairs grouped about low tables. The bar was at one end set inside an alcove, with high stools around it. An old piano stood to one side. Sarne lifted Tamsin on to a stool, his hard-fingered hands grasping her waist and, momentarily, lingering. He smiled, not only with his lips but with his warm, brown eyes. Her very bones began to melt under that regard. It was—almost—as if he meant it.

'Martini?' he asked, and when Tamsin nodded, he turned to the young man behind the bar.

Maybe, she thought, clasping her hands tightly on her lap and crossing her ankles on the footrest, maybe he did mean it—for now, for a month—or two. She must not let herself be fooled by man-ways. Desire, she told herself severely, was their chief motivation, not love. How could a man possibly love a woman after knowing her for—how long was it?—thirty-six hours?

No, she didn't trust him, not because she doubted his integrity, but simply because he was a man—and such a man! He pushed the drink along the bar top towards her and leant sideways against the counter, his foot lifted to the rest. A hand curled round his glass and he contemplated Tamsin with smiling eyes.

'How long is it?' he asked, echoing her thoughts. 'Thirty-six hours?'

'Since we've known each other? More or less,' Tamsin answered, sipping her drink.

'Unbelievable,' he murmured, then he grinned. 'I work fast, don't I?'

Her face grew serious and she stared into her glass. Somehow she must damp down the strange happiness that lit her face from inside, like the lights illuminating the swimming-pool outside. It couldn't have happened to her. She couldn't have fallen in love with a man she had known for only a day and a half! It was infatuation, that was all. She was flattered that such a man had singled her out, taken pity on her and kept her company, amusing himself now and then by kissing her.

'Now,' he said, draining his glass and ordering another drink, 'tomorrow is Monday. I shall show you Lugano, its mountains and valleys and its lakes. I shall take you sightseeing in my car wherever you want to go.' He raked in his pocket for money, put a handful down and waved the change away.

Tamsin stared at him. 'Are you sure? I mean, it's hardly fair of me to monopolise your time so much. There's no need——'

'There's every need. That way, I won't have to watch a lonely girl, a little sorry for herself, looking with envy at every family, every couple, young or old, who comes into her view.'

Tamsin took a gulp from her glass and choked. He

moved nearer, hit the upper part of her back with the palm of his hand and, when she was herself again, left his hand where it was.

'Sorry,' she murmured, wiping her eyes. She wriggled slightly, trying to indicate that she found his hand irritating, but he ignored her contortions. 'I'm sorry, too, for being so obvious.'

'You may be to me,' Sarne said, with a smile, 'but I doubt if you are to others.'

'What do you mean?' she asked sharply. 'That you possess greater perception than a mere tourist—because you aren't that, are you?—that you have a penetrating, psychological insight that your common-or-garden, simple-minded holidaymaker just doesn't possess?'

His smile broadened. 'Definitely.'

She smiled at him quickly and provocatively. 'You're modest, aren't you?'

'Very. I'm glad you've discovered that so early in our relationship. And stop being sarcastic, Miss Selby. It doesn't suit you.'

Tamsin coloured at his mild rebuke, then she frowned. 'Relationship? We aren't going to have a "relationship".'

His brows lifted slowly, cynically. 'No?'

'No! I told you, that's not——'

'Your way. You've said it so often, my sweet, you're boring me.'

'You're arrogant, supercilious and conceited. I'm going!' She swung the stool round and felt for the floor, but without the help of the foot rail, it was too far away. There were two alternatives—either she swung back and got down the easy way, or she slid ignominiously, and a little painfully, the long way down to the floor.

The problem was resolved by two strong hands on her shoulders spinning her back to face the bar. 'Stay where you are. We're going places together, so we have things to discuss.'

'We haven't! I'm not your responsibility. I chose to come here alone and I'm going to stay alone. I don't want company, thank you, especially yours!'

'Behave yourself, young woman, or I'll take you upstairs —to your room or mine, it doesn't matter to me—put you across my knee and give you the spanking you're asking for.' His eyes sparkled, his lips were tight.

Others who had drifted to the bar smiled at the altercation, and knowing that everything Sarne had said had been overheard, Tamsin's face flamed. She felt as if he had indeed chastised her in the way he had threatened, but it was her pride that smarted, not any part of her anatomy. Her lips trembled ominously and she pressed them together. He had humiliated her in front of others and she would not stay with him a moment longer.

'I'm tired, Mr Brand,' she said, and watched his eyes flicker at her use of his surname. 'I should like to go to bed.'

He nodded but did not attempt to help her down from the stool. 'I'll take you upstairs.'

'Please don't bother.' It was as if she had not spoken. He walked with her to the lift and pressed the button. When the door slid open, he motioned her in.

He leant against the back of the lift and folded his arms across his chest, eyeing her openly, taking in her satisfying shapeliness, the long, unruly curls, the firmly averted profile. She glanced at him—she couldn't help herself—and found him smiling. 'Forgiven me?' he asked.

'No.' Her shoulders straightened, her head lifted higher.

'You will,' he said softly, 'you will.'

At her door he took the key from her and turned it in the lock, but he held the door shut. 'Tomorrow we have a date. Remember?' She did not answer, her pride still stinging. A finger lifted her chin, forcing her eyes to his. 'Yes or no?'

It was the dark, ardent look she could not resist, the smile that softened the demanding lips, the charm that could make a glacier move faster.

'Yes,' she whispered.

Once again that evening she knew the touch of those lips. They brushed hers once, twice and left her wanting more. 'For the coming few days,' he said, 'we'll be just two people together. There'll be no past for us, the future won't matter. Only the present will exist, and we'll make the most—the utmost—of it. Agreed?'

She nodded. She could not have done otherwise. She was mesmerised by those familiar, yet unfamiliar, eyes.

'I'll call you tomorrow morning. When the telephone rings, wake up and answer it, won't you?' She smiled. '*Buona notte, cara,*' he murmured, and went away.

Tamsin sat on her bed. The brush of his lips still tingled on hers. The blood pounded through her veins. Then she remembered. *For the coming few days, we'll be two people together.* What would happen when those days were over? Would he be gone?

CHAPTER FOUR

TAMSIN was sleeping deeply when the telephone bell jangled its way into her dreams. She stirred and groped for the receiver, if only to silence the noise.

'Tamsin Selby here,' she answered, the words running sleepily into one another.

'Good morning,' the deep, male voice replied. 'This is your early-morning call.'

Tamsin peered at her watch. 'It's only seven-thirty. Couldn't you have let me sleep a bit longer?'

'Stop moaning! And what a way to greet a man, one

who's intending to sweep you off your feet into my car, into my company and at the end of the day, who knows, into my arms!'

Tamsin smiled. 'I'll settle for the car and the company.'

'She spurns my offer of love! She must be the first female who's done that since I tentatively tried out my masculine charms on the first of the countless women in my life.'

Tamsin clamped her teeth together and made no reply.

'Now I've made her jealous. If only I were there to see her face!'

'You haven't made me jealous, and if you don't tell me why you phoned me so early in the morning, I'll ring off.'

'And if you do, I'll come battering on your door until you're forced to open it.' Once again he had managed to silence her. 'Now,' he went on, 'if you'll go out on one of your balconies and look across to that mountain which rises behind the hotels and villas—it's called San Salvatore— you'll see where we two are going this morning. I'll give you fifteen minutes——'

'I've only just woken up!'

'Twenty minutes. Then I'll come and collect you and escort you down to breakfast.' He rang off before she could protest.

Tamsin swung out of bed, threw open the curtains and ran into the bathroom. It took her less than ten minutes to shower and dry herself. Then she selected from the many clothes in her wardrobe a short-sleeved, blue-patterned dress with a low-cut square neckline. The top was gathered into fullness and showed flatteringly the swelling lines of her breasts. Her hair, as usual, went its own way, curving forward over her cheeks and nestling round her throat.

The tap on the door, although expected, startled her and set her pulses racing. One last look in the mirror, then she crossed to the door and opened it. She had intended to walk straight out on to the landing, but the tall, broad-shouldered man outside barred her way. His navy towelling shirt was open-necked and short-sleeved, the hip-hugging belted slacks were dark-coloured, too.

Brown eyes looked down at her, trailing her face, figure and dress. A finger flicked at the fair curls which clustered round her long, pale throat. 'A pink-cheeked, beautiful, eager young blonde—mine for the next few days. What man could desire more?' Hands found her waist and he smiled. 'Do I get a good-morning kiss? Nothing involved, just a simple, straightforward meeting of the lips.' She stiffened. All the same, he impelled her towards him. Her stubborn body, however, stood firm.

'If you resist, *carina*,' he said, his eyes flashing a warning, 'you'll begin to arouse my passions. Surely your experience of your—how many was it?—two or three boy-friends has taught you that?'

'My "experience" of my boy-friends,' she hit back, 'was very——'

'Innocent? I bet!' His eyes mocked. 'With that face and that figure—do you really expect me to believe such lies?'

'Don't accuse me of lying!'

'Come, sweet Tamsin,' he smiled winningly, 'all I wanted was an aperitif, an appetiser. Let me demonstrate.' He drew her to him until her body touched his. Then his lips lowered and he pressed two gentle kisses on her pouting lips. 'You see? And all that fuss!'

They stood apart again, but his hands remained where they were, on her body, subtly, insinuatingly moving over the curves which meandered from armpits to hips. She wanted to brush those hands away because they disturbed her so, but heeded his warning and by drawing herself in, controlled her reactions.

'Why,' she asked, looking up at him, 'are you at times so —so, well, Italian?'

He threw back his head and his laughter echoed along the corridor. People, leaving their rooms to go down to breakfast, glanced their way and Tamsin felt embarrassed by what she imagined they must be thinking of her.

'Figure it out for yourself, girl. I'm half Italian, am I not? My mother is an Italian-Swiss, although her home is now in the States. My father was English, as I told you.'

'Was?'

'My mother's a widow.'

'I'm sorry.' He bowed his head in acknowledgement and released her, but immediately took her hand. They walked along and descended the marble staircase.

The head waiter greeted them with a broad smile, his dark eyes noting their linked hands. '*Buon giorno*, Signore Brand,' with a nod to Tamsin, '*signorina*. Breakfast is being taken on the terrace, it is such a beautiful day.'

Tamsin's eyes grew brighter at his comment. Strangely, it *was* a beautiful day, although she had scarcely had a chance to glance at the weather. Something inside told her just how beautiful it was—and it had hardly begun.

'A table for two, *signore*?' the head waiter asked.

'*Si*, Luigi, *per favore*.'

Luigi led them to a table at the end of the terrace where branches of the trees overhung the tables.

Breakfasting on fruit juice and flaking rolls, cheese, conserves and coffee, life for Tamsin seemed to have reached a pinnacle of happiness. Was it the sun, its rays already warm enough to flick at the bare skin; the greenery of the trees, firs, Corsican pine, lush palms; the blue of the lake forming a promising backcloth and revealed through the gently moving leaves and branches. Or was it the presence of the black-haired, keen-eyed man sitting opposite her, 'hers', as she was 'his' for the next few days?

'Are we going by car, Sarne?' Tamsin ventured, breaking the pleasant silence between them.

'By car—to Monte San Salvatore, when it's a mere walk away? Lazy little kitten, aren't you?' She went pink at his description and the familiarity wrapped up in it.

'No,' he went on, 'we walk to the foot of the mountain. There's a funicular railway to the top. It's nine hundred and twelve metres high. That is, around three thousand feet. Finished your breakfast?' He pushed back his chair and came round the table to pull out Tamsin's.

As she stood, she smiled at him, 'You're very polite. I'm not used to it.'

'So your English boy-friends aren't attentive?' Her smile was returned in full measure and her heart stood on its head. 'It must be my Italian inheritance coming out,' he said. 'You should see the "English" in me when it gets going. I warn you—on this holiday, steer clear of it. Cling to the "Italian" me. It's much more—amenable.' He held out his hand. 'Come, cling to it—hard.'

She did and laughed up into his face, oblivious of the interested stares. They passed the table at which the Dutch guests sat. They nodded good morning and Sarne exchanged a few words with them in Dutch. Tamsin wondered at his ability to switch from one language to another so fast. She supposed it was because he lived in Switzerland, a country of many languages. Or did he live there? She wished she knew. But she could not ask questions. No past, no future, only the present. They had made a pact and she must honour it.

The funicular railway was a one-coach train and was painted a vivid red. It made its way up and down the mountainside innumerable times a day filled with eager, excited people. It was a new experience for Tamsin. She gazed first out of one side then the other, admiring the view, astonished at the gradient and even putting her head through the windowless side to see how much higher they had to go—until a firm hand seized her shoulder and drew her back.

Sarne pulled her beside him and put his arm round her. He whispered in her ear, 'You're behaving just like those kids up there.' "Up there" meant the other people in the carriage who, because of the steepness of the gradient, were actually seated above them.

'I can't help being so interested,' she protested, enjoying the feel of his arm around her, his thigh pressing against hers. 'You've probably been in one of these things many times, but it's all new to me.'

'Go ahead,' he said, 'get excited. It's refreshing to see you that way. It makes me see things through your eyes, as if it were the first time for me.' A kiss feathered her cheek and she turned surprised, responsive eyes to him.

At the terminus, they climbed out of the funicular and climbed up to the viewing area. Tamsin caught her breath. Extending far into the distance was a view which delighted and awed. Below, dominating the panorama, was Lake Lugano, blue as the sky it reflected.

Pleasure steamers, ferry services, yachts, looked like specks on the water, their white trails like faint pencil marks. Across the lake was Monte Brè, the thickly populated mountain which, from the lakeside at night, had seemed to be magically illuminated from inside. Now, roads and villas and hotels could be seen clearly against its tree-covered surface.

'Across there,' two hands turned her head, 'if you look very hard, you can just see Lake Maggiore. Over there, the Lombardy Plain. In the far distance the Swiss Alps. Sometimes it's possible to see the Maritime Alps and the Appennines.'

Sarne urged her round to look in another direction. 'Down there is Melide, where there's a model of the whole of Switzerland in miniature. Across the bridge is Bissone. Farther along, Campione—a small piece of Italy inside Switzerland and known partly for its casino. Down there is Morcote, which is sometimes called the "pearl of Lugano". Amongst many other things, there's a fourteenth-century church there, where famous people are buried. The lake steamer calls there.'

'Now,' he smiled, 'having pointed out to an open-eyed young tourist some of the beauties in and around Lugano, I think I'm entitled to a drink to slake my thirst.' His eyes lingered on her upturned lips. 'Well,' with a smile, 'one of my thirsts. The other will have to wait to be satisfied at a more opportune moment.'

There were tables on a sun terrace overlooking the view. The tables and chairs were scarlet, the umbrellas of many colours. As Tamsin drank her coffee and Sarne his beer, Tamsin's eyes feasted on the grandeur, on the sweep of mountain ranges, lakes and white-flecked sky. The mountains were tree-covered and resembled green velvet, scarred here and there by roads and pathways running down to water level.

It was nearly lunchtime when they descended to Lugano in the funicular railway. It jolted and jerked and moved slowly down the steep gradient. At the station Sarne took Tamsin's hand.

'When we've eaten,' he promised, 'we'll go on a trip around the lake in the car.'

At the hotel, Sarne requested that his place be moved to Tamsin's table. He did remember, as the waiter carried out his instructions, to ask if she agreed to such a move. But it was plain that he had taken her acceptance as a foregone conclusion because the deed was accomplished almost before she had finished nodding her head.

They did not speak much as they ate their lunch. Tamsin was too happy just having Sarne sitting opposite her, too afraid to spoil the golden accord which had so miraculously established itself between them, to break the silence.

Sarne seemed preoccupied, looking around him but appearing not to see anything of the waiters' quick-footed movements, the pot plants which decorated the half-empty dining-room, the movement in the breeze of the colourful shrubs in the gardens beyond the windows.

Tamsin wished she could see into his mind. Her attentive, hand-holding companion of the morning seemed temporarily to have been swallowed up inside the thoughtful, remote, slightly daunting man who now shared her table.

His expression reminded her fleetingly of the look on his face the first moment she had met him. An autocrat, she had considered him, a man used to giving orders—and having them obeyed. She had thought at the time that he had classed her as 'inferior', but in the holiday atmosphere which encompassed them and in which their acquaintance had grown and developed—like the speeded-up life cycle of a plant in the heat of the desert—his attitude seemed to have undergone a subtle change.

Was it because, after seeing the quality of her clothes and guessing as a result—albeit wrongly—that her background was 'upper class', he had regarded her as fit to be admitted to his privileged world? In other words, she thought with some bitterness, was he not only arrogant, but also a snob?

'Your expression frightens me.' Sarne's voice was softly mocking, the brown eyes smiling. He had returned to her from the distant, untouchable areas of his mind. 'What terrible thoughts are you thinking? Does my behaviour really merit such a scowl?'

Her face cleared and she laughed, her head tilting back and revealing the whiteness of her throat. Around it was the gold necklace her mother had lent her for the duration of the holiday, the only really valuable piece of jewellery her mother possessed.

'That's better, *cara*. You should laugh more often. You become irresistible, not that you aren't even when you're serious, of course.'

Tamsin smiled and looked down to hide her confusion. 'Where did you learn the art of flattery, from the Italian side of your family or——'

'Certainly not the English! Have you ever known an Englishman flatter a woman?'

She pushed away her coffee cup and folded her napkin.

'In my book, flattery is false and insincere.'

'It was you who called my remarks about you "flattery".' His tone had a chill to it and she glanced at him apprehensively. Had she damaged that accord, were they back on different sides of the fence?

'I'm sorry.' Her eyes were down again. 'It's just that—well, I'm not used to compliments.'

'Unused to compliments? Unused to politeness? What kind of young men do you associate with?' He was smiling again and relief flooded over her.

In Sarne's car, after lunch, Tamsin found the traffic dense and frightening, although Sarne negotiated it with an ease which told of his familiarity with its fast-changing patterns. When they left the heavily-congested town centre behind and the road began to rise from the lakeside, Tamsin managed to unclench her hands and relax. Sarne laughed and teased her about her front-seat driving.

'You must have driven here many times to be able to negotiate all that traffic as well as you did,' she commented.

'Many times,' he replied laconically. Again, he was giving nothing away. They climbed the roads which wound around the sides of Monte Brè, and as their height increased so the beauties of the great bay were revealed more fully. The sun on the surface of the blue water cast light and shade across its swirls and eddies caused by passing boats. Round the bay stood the great rugged mountain which was San Salvatore, with its velvet-like green slopes and rough rock-ridged face dominating the scene.

Whenever it was possible, Sarne stopped the car so that Tamsin could take photographs.

'There's no time this afternoon, unfortunately,' he told her, 'to go to the summit of Monte Brè. It's three thousand feet high and on a clear day you can see the mountains of the Bernese Oberland and Valais, which are snow-covered all the time.'

Back in Lugano, Sarne parked his car and took Tamsin to the small but beautiful fifteenth-century church of Santa Maria degli Angioli. She gazed, catching her breath, at the astonishingly detailed frescoes which decorated the church. She looked for a long time at the bright freshness of the colours, the life and simulated movement in the great paintings, which had been so well preserved through the centuries.

They had tea at an open-air café across the road from the lake. Each table had its wide-spreading umbrella and brightly-coloured tablecloth which blew about in the breeze. The waitress was Italian and Sarne gave their order in that language. Again Tamsin marvelled at the ease with which this language, like so many others, flowed from his lips.

The sense of excitement had not left her. It was with her all the time, whenever she was by his side. These few days were a kind of dream and she was afraid that, if she pinched herself, she would wake up and find Sarne had gone. Now and then people passing would notice him and a hand would be raised in salute. He would salute back and sometimes exchange a few words—in German, French, even, Tamsin thought, Spanish.

He caught her look of astonishment and laughed, stretching out a hand and covering one of hers. 'Don't look so worried, my love. I'm still an Englishman at heart.'

'His love'! The expression came so easily from him she knew it meant nothing. But, part of her yearned, if only it were true! If he could go around with someone of the opposite sex as they had been doing and yet feel no deepening of the bond between them, then she could not.

Sarne settled the bill and led her, his hand entwined with hers, across the road to the lakeside. He gazed over the water to the distant mountains and for a few moments he seemed lost to the world—and, as Tamsin saw with sadness, to her, too. He seemed to have forgotten her, yet when his eyes swung her way and he caught the anxiety she could not disguise, he smiled, a warm, aware smile that made her wonder if his thoughts had been as far away as she had imagined.

'Don't look so scared, kitten. I won't desert you in the middle of a foreign land.' So his wish to brighten her solitude was, after all, the only reason for his interest in her these few fleeting days? Disappointment clouded her happiness, but she knew that she must at all costs hide it from his perceptive eyes.

'I never thought you would,' she responded as cheerfully as she could manage. 'I can usually tell when a—a person can be trusted,' she rushed on, 'and——'

'And I'm one of them?'

She nodded, feeling momentarily like a child with her hand in his—until she recalled his sarcasm that day in her room when he had thrown at her her 'clinging' ways. She snatched her hand from his and rubbed it against her hip.

He watched the action, astonished. 'Now what have I done?' She gazed up at him again, wishing he were not so tall and that she did not have to tilt her head back quite so far. What *had* he done? She moistened her lips. 'I—I just remembered—what you said about me the other evening...'

He made a gesture of impatience. 'Come on, you stupid little idiot.' He grasped her hand so tightly she winced. 'I thought we'd agreed to live for the day, the hour, the minute? No barriers of past or future——'

'I'm sorry. I'll try to remember. Or,' she said with a smile, 'should I say forget?'

Brown eyes searched the blue-grey ones, then he said abruptly, 'We're going on a lake steamer. There's one coming. If we hurry, we'll catch it.'

So hand in hand they ran, he with long easy strides, she with small quick steps, along the road towards the jetty. They arrived as the boat docked. At the kiosk Sarne spoke in Italian and two tickets were pushed towards him. He paid, smiling at the woman, and said, '*Grazie, signora.*'

The woman, plainly caught like so many others by his charm, smiled back. '*Prego, signore,*' she said.

Sarne rejoined Tamsin who asked, uncertainly, 'What was all that about?' He frowned and, afraid that he might think she was prying, added quickly, 'I wish I could speak Italian, or German, or——'

'I bought two tickets for the journey.' He grinned. 'Then I said "Thank you, *signora*," to which she replied, "You're welcome, sir." Satisfied?' She smiled back at him and he said, with glinting eyes, 'Are you getting so attached to me you're becoming jealous even when I ask for two tickets from a middle-aged woman?'

'Attached', 'clinging'—there was the implied accusation again. 'Jealous?' Tamsin snapped, taking him seriously although she told herself she was a fool to do so because she was only giving herself away. 'When I hardly know you, and when before very long, we'll be going our separate ways?'

She sounded so convincing she almost persuaded herself that what she was saying was true, that he didn't matter to her in the least, that saying goodbye to him would not tear at her very heartstrings ...

'All right, all right, you've made your point. Now, will you kindly stop talking and follow me.' He smiled provocatively. 'I like my women to be docile and submissive.'

Walking by his side over the gangplank which led on to the steamer, she asked, smiling up at him, 'Am I one of your women?'

He looked down at her. There was a strange expression in his eyes. 'Yes. For the moment.'

Her heart, having leapt like a newborn lamb, sank back into place like a tired sheep. 'For the moment,' until she had gone and the next one had come to take her place.

When the steamer moved from its moorings, her spirits revived. Sarne was here beside her, leaning against the rail, watching the rippling water as fascinatedly as she was. It was today that mattered. Even tomorrow was too far away to care about.

The boat made its way across the lake, calling at villages which were sometimes built so near the edge it was as if their feet were dabbling in the water. Jetties extended to receive and land passengers. Multi-storeyed apartment houses towered over the waterfront, vying for place with hotels which were bright with sunblinds and umbrellas over waterside tables.

Villas stood proudly on the hillsides, climbing the mountains as if in an effort to dissociate themselves from the tourists and holiday crowds. From the heat-mists, mountains rose and fell, tree-covered or bare rock, reflecting back the sun's rays.

Tamsin, with Sarne beside her, climbed to the upper deck and found a table near the side of the vessel, giving them an uninterrupted view of the passing scenery. A girl approached, holding a notepad.

She smiled. *'Was möchten Sie?'*

Sarne looked at Tamsin. 'Coffee?' She nodded and he replied, *'Zwei Kaffee, bitte.'*

When the girl had gone, Sarne smiled. 'For your information,' he said, 'she asked what we would like and I said two coffees, please.'

Tamsin laughed. 'Thanks for the lesson in "German for tourists".' She sighed. 'It's so comforting to have you around. Whatever language you're addressed in, you can speak it back.'

He shrugged and in the movement Tamsin could detect a touch of his Latin origins. 'It's a gift, as they say,' he said, and smiled his heart-melting smile. It turned just a little mocking as he asked, 'So you find me "comfortable" to be with, do you?'

He watched her closely and could not have missed the flush that warmed her cheeks. This man—a comfort? When her pulses raced and her very blood pounded through her veins at the sight, the feel of him, even the thought—let alone the touch—of his lips against hers.

'Yes,' she said, doing her utmost to sound convincing, 'nice and comforting and—and——' she *had* to put him off the scent, 'avuncular.'

The flicker that momentarily hooded his eyes had hers edging away to seek the blue of the lake all around them. Had she gone too far? But his next words reassured her.

He laughed and said, 'Call me Uncle Sarne, *Nichte!*' She frowned and he said, 'Shall I translate for the benefit of my little relation? The word means "niece".' So he had not been as annoyed as she thought at her statement.

The waitress returned with two cups of creamy coffee and Sarne, settling the bill, talked to her in her own language. The girl spoke volubly and seemed excited at what he was saying and counted on her fingers. She coloured, so he must have paid her a compliment—she was, after all, dark-haired and attractive—and she went away laughing.

'There now,' said Sarne, turning back with a satisfied expression to Tamsin, 'that must have got the jealousy chemistry in your body working overtime!'

'Don't keep calling me jealous,' she responded tartly. 'Where you're concerned,' she lied, 'it's simply not applicable.'

His smile was sardonic, but he said, 'We were discussing the subjects she's reading at Heidelberg University. Languages, she told me—quite a number, it seems.'

So he had paid the girl a compliment, Tamsin thought, drinking her coffee. 'Which means,' Tamsin said, 'that I could have given her the order in English and she would have understood?'

'She would. Yet you couldn't have understood her if she had addressed you in her own language, could you? Aren't you ashamed of yourself, niece?' he taunted. 'That's the trouble with the English. When they get into a foreign country they're lost unless someone comes to their rescue and speaks to them in the English language. Because around six hundred million people throughout the world speak English, they think that no matter where they go they'll be understood, regardless. Arrogant, aren't they?' he mocked.

She stirred her coffee unnecessarily. 'Don't you mean "us"? You're English, too.'

'Half.' He lifted his cup and drank. 'When I'm in my mother's home country, the Italian-Swiss half of me is dominant.' He smiled and his white teeth showed. 'The English half of me isn't nearly so pleasant as this one. Didn't I warn you?'

They were silent for a while. Tamsin listened to the chatter around her of other tourists and wished she could understand what they were saying. She made a vow that, on her return home, she would study a foreign language at an evening class. She couldn't come abroad again feeling as helpless as this—relying on other people's knowledge of English, on someone like Sarne Brand coming to her rescue. Next time, she told herself, and the thought was painful, there would be no dark-haired, brown-eyed, heart-breakingly good-looking man called Sarne Brand around at all ...

'Tamsin.' The word was a whisper, the lips that spoke it full, sensitive and disturbingly near. 'Come out into the moonlight from the dark corner your mind is huddled in.' She looked at him and could not control the faintest tremor of her lower lip. She hoped he did not notice it, but little, it seemed, escaped him. 'Tell me,' he coaxed, reaching out and touching her cheek.

Tell this man sitting opposite her, with his proud bearing, the magnetism of that charm, those eyes with their intelligence and incredible depths—tell him that she was *in love* with him? That she dreaded the day of their parting, that she could not allow herself to visualise her future life without him?

A finger trailed from her cheek to her neck, down, down

her bare throat to the low-cut neckline of her dress. It stopped in the centre and hooked round the elasticated top of the bodice, tugging on it and opening it wider. It was an intimate gesture, but she did nothing to stop it. Her skin tingled, her body tensed with longing, her eyes locked with his.

'*Cara*,' he whispered, 'will you dine with me tonight?'

Her throat was dry. 'At the—at the hotel?' He nodded. 'I should like to,' she told him.

'Good,' said Sarne, releasing her and holding out his hand. 'Walk with me, kitten.' They strolled hand in hand round the deck, saying nothing, pausing now and then to watch a passing boat or let their eyes climb to the mountain tops, shading their faces from the sun's dazzling rays.

Words were unnecessary. They sat together and Sarne's arm around her waist pulled her close. Of its own accord her head dropped to his shoulder and when she stole a look at him to see if he objected, she was met by a smile and a touch of his lips on hers.

'Cuddle up, *niece*,' he whispered. 'Let *uncle* make you comfortable.'

She laughed and pressed against him, remaining there for the rest of the journey back to Lugano.

There was a candlelight dinner at the hotel that evening. The crisp white tablecloths had been removed and red and white check table coverings had taken their place. The main lights had been switched off and on each table a tall, new candle stood in a holder. The curtains had been closed to keep out the sunlight and to create a romantic atmosphere.

When Tamsin came down the staircase, Sarne moved towards her from the reception desk against which he had been leaning. As always at the sight of him her heartbeats raced. He was dressed more formally, in a dark suit and pale blue shirt. The drape of the jacket emphasised his broad shoulders, the perfectly-cut trousers the leanness of his legs.

His manner was easy, his bearing commanding.

He held out his hand and Tamsin put hers into it. As before she looked up at him a little tremulously. How could she hide her admiration? He smiled down at her and led her into the darkened, shadow-filled dining-room.

It seemed that Sarne had asked for a table to be reserved for them. 'You look delectable,' he murmured as he motioned the waiter away and pulled out Tamsin's chair himself, waiting for her to be seated. 'Your wardrobe must be elastic. Every time I see you you're wearing something different.'

'That's because——' She stopped herself, glad that the candlelight would hide her heightened colour. She would have to be more careful. 'Because you—you only think I am,' she finished weakly.

He shook his head. 'I have an excellent memory for detail. Not,' he laughed, 'that a woman's clothes are a "detail".'

He eyed her gown. It was a pale blue, sleeveless and close-fitting to the waist. The deep neckline was edged with a large collar and revers. At the waist was a belt which tied into a bow and the skirt hung gracefully to the ankles. It had undoubtedly, even to the unpractised eye, cost a lot of money, and Sarne Brand's eye, Tamsin thought, acutely conscious of his appraisal, was certainly not that.

His gaze lifted to her face and hair and he smiled. 'I see your hair is still its untameable self.'

Tamsin's hand lifted nervously to smooth it. 'It's a nuisance. It has a mind of its own. Perhaps if I had it cut short——'

'Don't you dare!' The vehemence of the words astonished her. 'What's wrong with it? I can visualise no other style—or colour—to go with your perfect complexion or personality.'

'You're flattering me again.'

'Flattery she calls it! Don't you ever look in the mirror, girl?'

The head waiter approached and Sarne spoke to him, gesturing towards Tamsin and shaking his head. The head waiter looked at her, too, his eyes open wide. Then he, too, smiled and he spoke rapidly in Italian to Sarne, who laughed and said to Tamsin,

'Luigi thinks you're the most beautiful woman guest in the hotel.' Tamsin coloured and shook her head shyly. 'It's no use, Luigi,' Sarne said, 'any compliment you pay her she dismisses as flattery.'

'Flattery?' Luigi pretended to be hurt. 'Luigi,' he indicated himself, 'I never flatter a lady. I always tell truth.'

They laughed again and became serious as Sarne gave him the order. Luigi left them and there was silence between them for a while. Other people entered, among them the Dutch guests.

'It's as well,' they said, 'that the curtains are pulled. Outside it is raining very hard and the sky is black. There's thunder about, too.' They went on their way.

'If there's a storm,' Sarne commented, 'it will be worth watching. In this part of the world, they can be spectacular. When dinner is over, we'll watch it from my windows.'

'Why yours?' Tamsin asked without thinking, as the waiter placed the first course in front of her.

'Why?' responded Sarne, his eyes mocking. 'Would yours be better, then?' He smiled. 'Is it, perhaps, a subtle way of inviting me to your room, instead?'

Tamsin coloured deeply. 'Why do you always read more than I intend into what I say?'

'Always is a long time,' Sarne mused, 'and our acquaintance has, to date, been short.'

'You know what I mean,' Tamsin responded with a touch of irritation. Sarne looked at her but said nothing.

When the meal was over, they took the lift to the third floor. As they were swept upwards, Sarne stood, hands in pockets, legs apart to steady himself, and watched her. An enigmatic smile curved his lips and Tamsin's worried eyes searched his in a vain attempt to discover the source of his secret amusement.

Was this his way with all women or was there something about her that aroused his mockery and his desire to tease and taunt? Her eyes moved from his. No answer there. Anyway, she asked herself despondently, what was the use of trying to find one? She would never guess, nor would he ever tell. Their acquaintance would be too brief for either happening.

At the door of his room, Sarne stood back to allow Tamsin to enter. He closed the door and propped himself against it, hands still in pockets. Tamsin glanced around. The room, being sited in exactly the same situation as her own, should have seemed familiar, but there were a number of things that were different.

There was a circular table with four chairs grouped around it. The armchair was deeper and looked more comfortable. On a shelf was a television set. The pile of the carpet was deeper and on the wall hung a large gilt-framed mirror. There were two beds in an alcove and curtains which, when drawn across during the daytime, would conceal the beds.

Tamsin supposed that as a resident he would be entitled to more comforts and touches of luxury than the management would give to ordinary guests. She looked up and caught his eyes still fixed on her. She became confused and agitated. Why did he watch her so much?

'It—it should be the same as mine,' she said, indicating the room with her hand, 'yet somehow it's different.' His gaze did not flicker and she grew more embarrassed. 'Although it should be, shouldn't it, because it's in an identical position, on—on the corner of the building ...' She knew she was babbling. 'With—with two balconies, just like mine.' She tried the glass door, but it was locked and he made no attempt to come across and open it for her. 'It's just that it's higher up. Same view, same buildings, but——'

She looked round, willing him to speak, and caught a strange, brooding look in his eyes. Her heart began to pound and she felt stifled, trapped. An enormous roll of thunder rumbled and reverberated all around, echoing through the valleys and booming over the mountaintops.

The room grew dark, the distant hills were lost entirely in the rain-mist, while the nearer mountains became black and menacing. Streaks of lightning sliced jaggedly through the air and ran to earth; giant flashes lit up the violent scene, then darkness came again.

Tamsin felt Sarne beside her and as she shivered—with his nearness, but he thought it was fear of the storm—his arm lifted and came to rest across her shoulders. Rain rammed down on the roofs, beating on the green branches, pitting the surface of the swimming pool with its force. It ran down the road, emptying the streets. The thunder rolled, the lightning, in its fury, struck and struck again against the mountains.

He turned her abruptly and she saw that he had thrown aside his jacket. There was a storm in his eyes, his face, the tight lips. Seconds before they came together, she knew it would happen. The elements unleashed outside had released within him potent, primitive forces. His body was hard like the side of a mountain and the emotions aroused by their physical contact were like the lightning flashes searing the blackness beyond the windows and dazzling into momentary blindness the watching eyes.

Sarne kissed her, his lips exploring, possessive—and experimental, as if testing her response, her willingness to yield. The reserve he had shown before and which had until now prevailed in the kisses he had given her had been cast aside and she fought for breath as though she had been climbing a mountain.

At length he held her away, looking deep into her eyes. The storm roared overhead. Flashes of lightning illuminated the room. He said, his jaw hard and jutting, his features angled and sharp in the intermittent flashes,

'I see no signal at red, no sign in your face telling me to stop.'

His hand fastened on to her throat and his mouth twisted and came down again. She swayed towards him, parting her lips willingly to receive his, and he proceeded to take the last of her breath from her body.

Perhaps he felt her fatigue, because his kisses slowly gentled and ceased. He released her, only to reach for her again, and her head came to rest against him, finding sanctuary, cheek to his chest. The thump of his heart was loud in her ear and she clung to his waist for support.

'So I'm comfortable, am I?' she heard him growl. 'So I'm avuncular, eh? It's a wonder you didn't insult me by calling me paternal or brotherly.'

So this was revenge for her comments earlier in the day. This lovemaking was nothing more than retribution. He eased her from him and lifted hands to smooth his hair. He straightened his tie and went across the room to the minibar, unlocking it and bending down to inspect the contents.

As the storm receded, grumbling, into the distance, it became lighter and the false night dispersed with the storm. A small patch of sunlight behind the mountains grew until it illuminated the whole sky. It turned the lake into liquid gold and reflected brilliantly from the walls of the hotels and villas. A few boats ventured out on to the water.

A glass was pushed into Tamsin's hand and she turned to face Sarne. The warmth was back in his eyes, like the sunlight after the storm, but there was a new look there. It was as though the barrier which had existed in their strangely tenuous relationship had been demolished and they now shared a knowledge of each other which nothing could erase from their minds. As though they had made love completely and totally ...

Sarne raised his glass. 'To us, to—shall I whisper the words?—the future.'

The future? There was none as far as they were concerned. Had he forgotten?

Tamsin shook her head, but drank with him all the same. 'There's only the present, Sarne. We agreed.'

He smiled. 'There's always the present. Yesterday was "today". Tomorrow will be "today". Now, what shall we do tomorrow?'

They laughed and he put down his glass, taking hers away. He led her across the room and sank into the depths of an armchair, pulling her on to his lap.

'Lie still, my love,' he said, 'just lie still.' Her cheek found his chest again and his arms went round her. His head rested against the back of the chair and there was only the sound of the thunder rolling into the distance.

After a while he moved, lifting his head and looking down at her. He fingered the necklace round her neck, touching her skin in a caressing way, and a tremor went through her body at the intimate gesture.

'Gold,' he said. 'An expensive woman, aren't you?'

It became vital that she should tell him the truth about herself—she held her breath. Why? This acquaintance—she could still think of no other name for it—had two, or was it three, more days to run. He need know no more about her than he knew now.

'The necklace is my mother's.'

'So it's true. They have money, and to spare, judging by this.' He let the necklace fall against her.

She had given the wrong impression after all. 'It's her only valuable piece of jewellery,' Tamsin hastened to say, but it was plain Sarne did not believe her. 'She inherited it from someone in her family.'

'I see. A family heirloom, no doubt.'

She lifted her head to protest, but it sank against his chest again. What was the use? And what did it matter? She sighed.

'What,' said Sarne, teasing, 'impatient for more kisses?'

Tamsin pulled herself upright. The question made her sound cheap, as though that was why she had come. 'I must go.'

He stood, pushing back his shoulders, then putting his hands on to her shoulders and pulling her round. 'Must you?'

Her eyes fell from his. 'Yes,' she whispered, looking for her handbag and finding it on the floor near the window where he had kissed her. She opened her purse. 'Please tell me how much I owe you.' His eyebrows rose and there was that glimpse again of the autocrat. The love had gone. 'For —for the drink you gave me.'

'You're not serious?'

'It says on the door of the mini-bar how much each drink is, I know that from my own. So——'

In a stride he was in front of her, kissing her again, his hands on her hips, pulling her against his thighs. When he put her from him, her colour was high.

'You've paid me, *carina*.' He smiled and lifted her chin. 'Better than all the money in the world.'

At the door she paused. Before she could stop herself, she asked, 'Tomorrow, Sarne ... ?'

'So you still want my company.' A hand ruffled her hair. 'We'll decide that in the morning. I'll call you first thing before breakfast.'

Sensitive as she was to their finely-balanced, fragile relationship, the answer seemed evasive. Was he already wishing himself free of their involvement? She grew angry with herself for having asked, feeling that she had thrown herself at him.

He walked with her to the lift and as they descended to

the first floor, they stood apart, but as before, his eyes did not leave her. As before, she could not hold his gaze. Outside her door, he lifted her hand, putting his lips to her wrist.

He smiled mockingly as he lowered her hand. 'It's the Latin in me,' he murmured, walking away with a brief salute.

CHAPTER FIVE

ALL night Sarne's kiss was with her. It was as though she had slept curled in his arms. When she awoke, she rejoiced that her watch told her it was time to get up. It meant that before long she would see Sarne again.

She showered and put on her sundress. This time he would not be able to say he had not seen the dress before. Over it she pulled a short matching jacket. Then, since there was nothing else to do, she sat on the bed and waited. She waited until it was long past the moment when the telephone had rung before.

A niggling worry began at the back of her mind. Had she been correct in her intuitive feeling last night that he had had enough of her? Was he trying to let her down gently by giving her the hint in a subtle way, by 'forgetting' to call her?

Breakfasts were well on their way by now. It was no use waiting, she would have to go down without him. As she closed her door and walked along the landing, she realised with amazement that her feet were taking her past the top of the stairs and towards the lift.

Well, why not? Why not call on Sarne and give him a surprise? If he was not fully clothed, he would tell her to wait. Or if he was not there, he wouldn't reply, would he?

What harm could there be in paying him a friendly call?

Outside his door, she lifted a hand—and paused. It was one thing to recall that passionate kiss. It was another to remember that vague but undeniable restraint which had manifested itself between them just before he left her. No, she thought, smiling, she must have imagined it! No man could kiss a girl as he had kissed her, then proceed to pass her off as just another romantic encounter.

The knock was timid, bringing no audible reply, so Tamsin tried again, becoming bolder. The door was not opened, but there was the sound of a raised voice saying, '*Herein!*'

Tamsin stood indecisively. The voice came again. '*Kommen Sie herein!*' This was followed almost immediately by, 'Come in, for heaven's sake, whoever it is. The door's on the catch.'

Sarne was fully dressed, seated on the side of the unmade bed, the telephone receiver to his ear. His eyes widened and his hand covered the mouthpiece. 'Tamsin, forgive me, I——' He spoke into the telephone. '*Un attimo, per favore*——' He patted the bed. 'Come here, *cara*, beside me.'

His hand came out. In the circumstances, she had to obey. Anyway, she had no wish to disobey. The mere sight of him had her thoughts in chaos. As she lowered herself beside him, his arm went round her. 'I won't be long.' To the caller on the telephone, '*Si*, Vincenzo?'

Tamsin hardly dared to breathe in case the arm around her was removed. She looked round the room. The curtains which in the daytime hid the beds were open. On the table was an empty tray. It seemed that morning tea had been served to him.

As Sarne spoke in fast Italian, his hand began a caressing movement down to her hip and up, up, above her waist until it encountered her breast, where it rested possessively. Tamsin knew she could have pulled his hand away, but her body was coming alive under his expert touch. She wanted him to go on caressing her until—— Her head turned and she encountered his eyes. He was still talking, but the fact that he was as aware of her as she was of him showed in the warmth of his smile.

His hand lifted to the back of her head, pressing it towards him so that his mouth, while he listened to the speaker at the end of the line, was within touching distance of hers. Their lips met in a soundless kiss, then his arm went to her waist and he carried on the conversation as if nothing had happened.

Tamsin marvelled at his ability to make love to a woman in the midst of what sounded like a business conversation. Which proved, she thought unhappily, how a man could separate, with no effort at all, his emotions from his intellect. A woman, the emotions, even lovemaking itself, took second place in a man's mind. Love, and women, were an indulgence, a pleasant pastime. Business, intellectual thought, work in whatever form, came first every time.

'*Arrivederci. Si*, Vincenzo, *a più tardi*.' The phone call finished, Sarne pulled Tamsin to stand in front of him and his arms linked round her waist. He smiled. 'Forgive me, *signorina*, for neglecting you. It should have been the other way round. I should have come to your room.'

'I'm sorry for intruding,' she said, 'but I—I didn't know what to do. You said you'd call me——'

'And the phone didn't ring. So you waited, hung around, sat down, stood up—then made the great decision. You would batter down my door and make your presence felt!'

She laughed shyly. 'Not really. I——'

His smile faded. 'I was just about to dial your extension when the phone rang. I'm afraid, my love, our plans will have to be changed.'

Tamsin frowned, her fingers feeling the texture of his tie. 'You mean for today, or——?'

'For today *and* the next two days. Our time together has

unfortunately shrunk to two and a half days.' Tamsin pressed her lips together, but he had caught the tremble. 'I'm as sorry as you are, sweet.' He pulled her beside him on the bed again, his arm still round her. 'You've probably seen the *palazzo dei congressi* mentioned in the guide book? It's a convention centre where national and international conferences are held. You're frowning. Why?'

'I can't quite see where you come in.'

He pushed at her chin playfully with his fist. 'Give me a chance to tell you, sweet.' He bent forward and his lips touched hers. He grinned. 'Sorry, I couldn't resist that. They were there for the taking.'

Her heart, already beating fast, began to race. Their knees touched and she wanted to stretch out her hand and touch him. It was then that she noticed with dismay how formally he was dressed. The crease in his trousers was knife-sharp. The material from which they were made had plainly cost a great deal of money. The jacket which matched them was draped on a chair.

'I—er'—he seemed to be having difficulty in conveying some information—'I'm a bit of an expert in languages. I speak—a few quite fluently.'

'I have noticed,' she said, with a slight smile.

He laughed. 'Well, the day after tomorrow, there's a week-long international conference starting at the convention centre. Something to do with the pollution of the world's waterways. One of the interpreters they've booked is ill and the organisers—they know me well—have asked me to take his place. Since my name is permanently on the list as a substitute interpreter when I'm in Lugano, I can hardly refuse, can I?'

Her heart sank. She shook her head. 'If you've volunteered——'

'It's hardly voluntary work,' he said dryly. 'I shall get paid, and well. Not that I need the money.'

She looked at him sharply. It had been a quick lift of the

curtain on to his private life, then, tantalisingly, the curtain had been dropped back into place.

'Don't look so forlorn, my love. It's only for just over a week, and then—then,' a shrug, 'well, the rest is up to you. Either we take it from where we are now, or——'

They stood. She could have taken him up on the unfinished sentence, but she did not. He was making it very clear that he considered it was she who was doing the running—after him. Also that, in his eyes, it was purely and simply a holiday affair, no more, no less. Why had she been such a fool as to let her emotions—no, worse, her heart, become involved?

Hadn't there been, from the start, something that had troubled her about the man, something that was different— elusively so—about him? And hadn't he done his best to hide from her all knowledge of whatever that 'something' was? A man and a girl. No past, no future. Only today.

He looked at his watch. Already he was becoming withdrawn into his own—his real—world. 'Time for breakfast, I think.' His hands closed on the sides of her head and tilted it upwards. 'Smile, sweet. It's not the end of the world. This morning I must go to the conference hall and discuss arrangements with the organisers. This afternoon and evening—and night?' with a smile, 'are ours. They belong to us.'

'Tomorrow?'

His hands fell away. 'Tomorrow I must work on the subject matter, get myself acquainted with the technical terms, translating them into the various languages I might be called on to interpret. The day after that, the conference begins and then, I'm afraid, I won't be seen much on the premises. After each day's session, the delegates like to mix and talk. I, as an interpreter, have to be there much of the time.'

There was a small silence. He pulled on his jacket and took her hand to lead her to the door. 'I'll be alone again.'

The words made their way through her lips before she knew they were even in her mind.

'I'm sorry, pet. That's life.' Another silence. 'You'll make friends. There are the van Ruyters, the Dutch couple. They're very pleasant people. They'll take pity on you.'

Was that what he had done—taken pity on her? She attempted to free her hand, but he clung all the tighter. 'We're breakfasting together,' he said firmly. 'We'll lunch together, too. After that, we'll do whatever you want.'

His door closed and they went down to breakfast hand in hand.

Without Sarne, the morning dragged. Tamsin went to the shops and bought some postcards. She returned to her room and wrote on them, one to her parents, one to her uncle, others to her friends. Then there was nothing else to do but go out and post them.

The lake shimmered in the sun which shone relentlessly from a cloudless sky. Tamsin carried the jacket of her sundress and felt the sun's rays burning her skin. She was glad she had covered herself with suntan lotion that morning. Her back and arms were browning nicely.

In the warmth, her body felt content, the accident that had initiated the holiday almost forgotten. If only her mind would leave her alone, if only her thoughts did not keep nagging at her, asking, Where's Sarne now? What is he doing? Are there any attractive women—— Then she pulled herself up. Sarne Brand was not hers to fret about. If there were a queue of women waiting for his favours, there would be nothing she could do about it.

The van Ruyters were out. In the lounge guests came and went. One or two smiled, others ignored her as she sat, flicking through magazines. She could have gone to her room, but there was more chance in the lounge of seeing Sarne whenever he came in. Her watch told her that in twenty minutes it would be time for lunches to be served.

'We'll lunch together,' Sarne had said. She would wait for him to return.

In the end she had to give in, wearying of looking up with anticipation every time the swing doors opened and closed, tiring of hoping and being constantly disappointed. The head waiter showed her to a table near the window and she saw that it was for one. When she had given her order, she shrugged. What did it matter if there was no place for Sarne? He wouldn't come now.

But he did come. When Tamsin saw him at the door, standing so tall and commanding, his dark eyes searching, searching for someone, something, her heart tilted like the earth knocked off its axis. When her eyes cleared, they saw that Sarne was making for her table, his long strides bringing him across the length of room that divided them.

He pulled out the chair which was opposite her and reached for her hand. He did not apologise. 'I thought I'd never get here.' There was energy and vitality in his whole bearing, an alertness of the eyes which told of a brain that had been busy and which still had not stopped working, of a morning spent in intellectual activity which had stimulated and challenged him. Challenged him—that was something she had never done. She had been there for the taking, as he had described her lips that morning.

A waiter hovered and Sarne released Tamsin's hand. The waiter set out the cutlery in front of Sarne, asking for his order. When the waiter had gone, Sarne said,

'It was good to get back and find you here waiting for me.'

A simple statement with an abundance of hidden meaning—or none at all, depending on how you looked at it. Was he pleased that it was *she* who had been waiting, or had it simply pleased his masculine pride?

She remembered how eagerly she had watched him approaching, how she had not bothered to hide her happiness that he had come at last.

'I'm sorry,' she said, sipping the fruit juice the waiter had brought, 'did I make myself so obvious? If I'm being a nuisance to you, if I'm "fastening on" to you, as you said the other day, if I'm following you about like a'—she tried to remember his words—'like a pet dog following its beloved master, just tell me and I'll go away. I'll never trouble you again.'

Narrowed eyes met hers. 'My word, you must be hungry!' The waiter came with the first course. 'Feed her, Giovanni, feed the girl. She's biting my head off. If you're not quick, she'll make a meal of me instead of that.' He indicated the food on the side table. The waiter laughed and proceeded to fill Tamsin's plate.

Tamsin coloured and could not meet Sarne's eyes. When at last they were alone again, she apologised. He brushed the apology aside and they ate in silence for a while.

At last he said, 'Feeling better now? Was your morning so terrible? Were you lonely?'

'Of course not,' she lied. 'I wrote cards and letters. I went out to post them.' *I watched for you and you never came* ... She did not speak the words aloud.

He gave her a quick, sceptical look but did not speak. Later, he said, 'I'm a wanted man, Tamsin. They need my help badly. They were short of two interpreters, not just one, so I'm doing my best to fill both vacancies.'

She frowned, showing her concern. 'Won't it be difficult?'

'Very. But I'll manage. I've had enough practice in the past.'

'Is that your—your work? Are you a professional interpreter?'

He looked at her speculatively over the rim of his glass of water. The look he gave her was not softened by warmth. 'If you mean is it my career and my livelihood, the answer's no.'

So she had transgressed again into his privacy. She must

watch herself more closely. She hated—and, she had to admit, feared—the side to him she did not know and which he never revealed.

'Cling to the Italian in me this holiday,' he had said. 'I warn you, steer clear of my English side.' Well, she had had her warning. She would take heed of it from now on.

They spent the afternoon by the swimming pool. When Sarne had called for Tamsin, he had worn a towelling robe, tied at the waist. She had no such cover to put over her scarlet bikini, but as Sarne's eyes wandered appreciatively all over her, she wished she had.

'I could eat you in that outfit,' he said, leaning lazily against the door. 'If I growl now and then, you'd better take cover.'

She unrolled her towel and flung it round her shoulders, trying to hide her slim form beneath its folds. He laughed and said, 'That only whets my appetite. It's a masculine trait to want to find out what's underneath. Come along, mermaid, before I turn into a giant whale and swallow you whole.'

It was so hot outside that extra covering became superfluous. Tamsin pulled the towel from around her and draped it over the back of the sun lounger. Sarne took off his robe and dropped it to the ground beside the folding chair next to Tamsin's.

A quick glance told her that his eyes were on her. Painfully conscious of the large areas of her body which were uncovered, she ran to the steps which led into the water, descended them swiftly and plunged in.

She turned on to her back, closed her eyes and swam for a while, arms lifting and falling, fair hair spread out behind her. Would Sarne join her? Her eyes opened and she turned her head. Was he talking to Mr and Mrs van Ruyter to whom they had waved as they sunbathed beside the pool?

He was at the edge, hands on hips, legs apart, smiling

down at her. She grasped the rail, pushed the hair from her eyes and gazed up at him, acutely aware of his intense masculinity. His swimming briefs were blue with a white stripe at each side. It was the first time she had seen him without the vaguely executive air which seemed to surround his personality wherever he went, whatever the circumstances might be.

It had even been there that afternoon in her room when he had tested the limits she had set upon how far she would allow a man to go with her. Even when he had been suggesting an intimate relationship there had been something aloof about him, aristocratic, imperious.

In the intervening few days, when they had come to know each other better—or so she thought—that manner had submerged and Tamsin had come to wonder if she had imagined it. But last night, when they had parted, she had acknowledged that it had not been imagination. The 'other man' in him was there, no doubt about it.

'Hi, sea maiden,' he said, squatting on his haunches so as to be nearer to her. 'Tempt me in, lure me to my doom, like the Lorelei.'

She laughed, her eyes dazzled by the sun and by the magnetism of the man. Those broad shoulders tantalised, the hair-covered chest invited hands to explore the dark jungle, the muscle-tough arms implanted a desire to be crushed by them. He stood again and there was no mistaking his overpowering maleness. Tamsin closed her eyes and tried to reason away the feelings within her that clamoured to be recognised.

There was a great splash and the wash of Sarne's impact on the water threatened to engulf her. She spluttered and strong hands lifted her by the armpits, keeping her afloat. In the confusion and excitement of the swimming pool, instincts need not be suppressed, free rein could be given to primitive impulses.

So when arms grasped Tamsin's body, admitting no

limitations on where they might hold her, when beneath the blue water hands moved over her midriff and breasts, she did not resist the intimacy. When lips found her own she gave them up as though it was his right to savour them to the full.

'I'll get beneath that English reserve,' she heard him murmur against her mouth, 'even if it kills me!'

So that was what she meant to him—a challenge to his male need to dominate and conquer! Tamsin wriggled and squirmed and because of the wetness her body slipped out of his hands. She turned on to her front and struck out, arm over arm, to the other end of the pool.

He followed, but there were too many people in the way. She was caught at last by the limitations of the pool, but when he had almost reached her, she dived underneath the other swimmers and eluded him, making for the steps. She was up them in no time and wrapping the towel about her.

When at last Sarne came out, his body glistening, she was laughing at him and her eyes were dancing with delight at having escaped.

He dried his arms roughly with a towel he had taken from his robe pocket. He looked down at her as she sprawled, still out of breath, in the sun lounger.

'You think you've won, don't you?' he said. 'Well, you can think again, my girl. I'll get you yet.'

'I thought,' she said sweetly, smiling up at him, 'you never did the running? I quote——'

'Okay, so you quote. You know what I meant—in the metaphorical sense. In reality, I love a chase if only because I can run so much faster. And I invariably catch my prey. Take heed, *signorina*. As I've said before, it's the Italian in me.' He flung himself into a chair beside her, then looked down at her recumbent form. His eyes, taking their time, slid over her long legs, her thighs, the fullness of her breasts, reaching her face at last. He smiled at the colour in her cheeks, knowing that it was not only the sun's rays that had put it there.

'You look a mess,' he said. 'Your hair——' He reached over to ruffle it, but she moved swiftly and evaded him, catching his hand before it reached its target. Her teeth moved towards his knuckles, but as they made sharp contact with his skin he jerked his hand away, crouching over her and catching a handful of her hair. She shrieked and he said,

'You vicious little brat! If you're asking for what I think you're asking for, you'll get it before the night's out. So behave yourself, or——'

'I'm sorry, Sarne, I'm sorry.' Her animation was subsiding, her natural reserve asserting itself as the stimulus of the swim, the caresses and the subsequent pursuit died down.

He seemed mollified by her apology and left her alone. He bent to pull out of the other pocket of his robe a pair of sunglasses and pushed them on. Behind them, his personality took on an air of mystery. With the warmth and fire of his eyes hidden from view, the remoteness returned, tantalising and daunting.

A cloud passed across the sun and Tamsin shivered. Sarne noticed at once.

'You'd better put some clothes on—for more reasons than one. If you lie like that beside me much longer...' She was up and gathering her things before he had finished the sentence. He stood, too, but she said,

'There's no need for you to come.' It seemed that her words, far from dissuading him, had had the opposite effect.

He did go with her, his robe over his arm, into the hotel and across to the lift. As they ascended, they eyed each other, he uninhibitedly as if the figure she presented was to him like a famous painting to a connoisseur—something to be studied in minute detail, with admiration for its perfection and for its freedom from flaws; she like an inexperienced swimmer watching terrified as an enormous wave comes slowly onward and which she knows will totally engulf her.

The first floor seemed a long way up. When the doors slid open, Tamsin said, 'Goodbye, Sarne.' Would he step out of the lift with her or would he continue to the third floor?

He smiled and bowed deeply. *'Buon giorno, signorina.'* The lift doors closed, shutting him from sight.

Tamsin entered her room with a feeling of disappointment. She could not deny that part of her had hoped he would see her to her room. Nor had he said a word about their meeting again before he began his work next day.

She put on a sundress, a strapless one this time, with an elasticated top. Her hair felt tangled so she went into the bathroom, sat at the mirror and looked at herself. So she was 'a mess', was she? Furious with Sarne for telling her so, she pulled the comb through her hair, screwing up her face with pain as the teeth caught in the fair tangles.

There was a noise in her room and she turned to see Sarne at the door of the bathroom. 'The catch was up, so I walked in,' he said, smiling.

Her heart, as usual, pounded at the sight of him. 'You— you can't come in here.'

Eyebrows lifted as if her denial of his right of entry to her bathroom surprised him. 'Sorry, *cara*, but I'm already in.' He sat on the edge of the bath and watched her reflection in the mirror.

Tamsin could see his reflection, too. His shirt was semi-transparent, showing clearly the outline of his body and even the dark area of hair on his chest. The sleeves were rolled up, the top buttons undone. His white slacks were close-fitting, revealing his leanness and hard-boned hips. He folded his arms and crossed his long legs, as if prepared to wait an eternity.

Under his unwavering surveillance, she applied her make-up. 'What the blazes are you putting all that stuff on your face for?' Tamsin did not reply, just went on applying it. After a few moments, as if he could not stand it any longer, he came to her side.

'Have you got some terrible skin defect I don't know about?' he asked irritably. 'Are there premature wrinkles, a crop of spots lingering on from adolescence? Is that why you're plastering a perfect skin with all that stuff?' She frowned, putting down the mascara she had been about to put on her lashes. 'Look at me, Tamsin.'

Resolutely, she kept her face averted. A hand came out and seized her chin, easing it round. Eyes scanned her features, once, twice, coming to rest at last on her lips, touched with pale pink lipstick. Slowly his mouth came down, meeting hers, resting, lingering, lifting.

She had had time to refuse the kiss, but their relationship had passed beyond that stage. He was no fool. He must know by now, she told herself, that any time he cared to kiss—and caress—her, no barriers would be erected by her. His lips, his hands could become as possessive as they liked, she would raise no objections. He stayed there, looking down at her.

Confusion stained her cheeks. 'You—you've got lipstick on your mouth.'

He smiled. 'Wipe it away for me.'

She found a tissue and reaching up, gently rubbed it round his lips. It was an intimate action, as though already their lovemaking had passed beyond the first stage into a more passionate involvement.

'Thanks, kitten.' He straightened. 'You shouldn't wear the stuff, then you wouldn't plaster me with it.' As though the temptation was too great, his palms feathered over her bare shoulders. He must have felt the faint tremble of her body at his touch, but he did not outwardly register the fact. He wandered into the bedroom.

When Tamsin followed, he was on the balcony, stretched out on one of the sun loungers. 'An hour or two before dinner,' he said. 'Let's stay here. I need all the relaxation I can get before the deluge tomorrow.'

Tamsin lay next to him on the other sun lounger. 'Will it be very hard work?'

'Very.' He did not elaborate.

Inexplicably she felt snubbed, as though he were shutting her out. And she knew better now than to question him further. If he put on mental dark glasses where anything other than his holiday self was concerned, then let him stay behind them. She had been warned by him often enough—'keep out'. And like an unwelcome caller being bayed at by ferocious dogs, she kept out, ready at any moment to turn and run.

Out of the silence, interspersed with cries from the pool, and the noise of traffic on the main road, Sarne said, 'Tell me about your family.'

The question shook her. Should she tell *him*, 'Keep out. You're prying into *my* affairs, into things which are no concern of yours'?

She did not have it in her to retaliate in kind. Her feelings for the man had, disastrously, gone too deep to give him pain by a tart reprimand. It was not in her to tell him, 'Mind your own business!'

'There's not much to tell. There's just me. And my parents, of course.'

'Does your father work for his living?' It was asked with studied casualness.

Her head turned sharply. 'Of course he does! How do you think we——' She had to be careful. Wasn't she here, in a luxury hotel, 'loaded' with Swiss francs, as she had told him? Also he knew she did not work, although not the reason for the lack of a job. He believed she had come from a rich background, otherwise how else had she been able to afford the holiday? There must be no word of being subsidised by her wealthy uncle, chairman of the company which owned the hotel.

Sarne was looking at her now, as if awaiting with interest her next statement.

'He's an electrical engineer,' she said flatly, 'working in local government.' Now he had the truth. How would he react?

There was a pause, then, 'Is it a managerial job?'

'More—more supervisory than managerial, I think. He's not terribly high in the hierarchy.'

She looked at him. Now he knew all. How had he taken the information? His eyes were closed, his head resting on the cushioned back. He had unbuttoned his shirt to allow the sun to enrich the tan which already covered his skin. His long lashes curled, his straight, firm nose made her want to lean over and run a finger down it, to bump over those thick, sensual lips.

'So where,' he said slowly, as if trying to work matters out, 'does the——' He stopped, as she had done.

'Money come from?' she finished for him. 'Now it's my turn to tell you to shut up, Mr Brand,' she said tartly. 'No past, we agreed, no future?'

'All right. So you don't want to tell me.' She shook her head. I'd like to, she longed to tell him, but I'm not allowed. My uncle said, Tell no one. Sarne inspected her narrowly, then looked out over the mountains.

'Strange,' Tamsin heard him murmur, 'I could have sworn you were on the level.'

She could not let that pass. 'I *am* on the level,' she cried, sitting forward.

'Look, sweetie,' he said lazily, 'calm down. I said I wanted to relax. Give me your hand.' Because she wanted to touch him so much, she obeyed. He clasped it, entwining their fingers. 'You don't need to tell me any more about yourself, nothing at all.'

Tamsin did not bother to work out why her heart sank at his words. She only knew it did. They sat, hand in hand, until he left her to dress for dinner.

Accept 'Give Us Forever' and 'Cloud Over Paradise' **FREE** as your introduction to **HARLEQUIN** SuperRomance.

Here's your chance to be among the first to enjoy two brilliant and sensuous new novels – absolutely FREE! They're your introduction to a brand new romance collection from Harlequin – America's leading Romance Publisher – and they offer more spellbinding involvement than you ever thought possible.

Turn the page and discover how 'Give Us Forever' and 'Cloud Over Paradise' can be yours FREE!

See over for your FREE BOOKS

Do not affix postage stamps if posted in Gt. Britain, Channel Islands or N. Ireland.

BR Licence No. CN81

Mills & Boon/Harlequin Reader Service
PO Box 236
Thornton Road
CROYDON
CR9 9EL

2

These blockbuster novels have taken America by storm – millions of copies have already been sold!

We're so convinced that you'll find 'Cloud Over Paradise' and 'Give Us Forever' absolutely irresistible that we'll send you, at the same time, the next two novels in the Harlequin SuperRomance collection, 'Captive of Desire' and 'Passion's Triumph', for just £1.75 each, postage and packing free. Each book is a gripping 380 pages long – that's real value! If you decide not to keep these two super books, send them back within 10 days and you owe nothing.

If you decide to keep them, we will send you the four latest Harlequin Super Romances each month, postage and packing free, *and always on 10 days approval. Whatever you decide, the first two books are yours to keep.*

It's an opportunity too good to miss!

'Cloud Over Paradise' and 'Give Us Forever' are the first novels in a major new series – enthralling and exciting stories of love and life that will leave you breathless.

Send for yours today – accept this offer by filling in the card below and POST TODAY!

Mills & Boon/Harlequin Reader Service, PO Box 236, Croydon, Surrey CR9 9EL

Enjoy over 380 pages of sensuous excitement in each book!

Yes, please send me 'Cloud Over Paradise' and 'Give Us Forever' FREE which I may keep whether or not I subscribe to Harlequin SuperRomances. I understand you will also send me 'Captive of Desire' and 'Passions Triumph' which I can keep for only £1.75 each (postage and packing free), or return to you within 10 days and pay nothing. Thereafter you will send me 4 Harlequin SuperRomance novels each month, on approval. I may keep these for just £1.75 each (postage and packing free). If I decide to close my subscription I shall write to you within 10 days of receiving my monthly parcel of books. I am over 18 years of age.

Please write in BLOCK CAPITALS

Name_____

Address_____

_____ Postcode_____

Signature_____

Orders returned without a signature will not be accepted. One offer per household. Offer applies in UK only – overseas send for details. If price changes are necessary you will be notified.

SEND NO MONEY – TAKE NO RISKS   5C3FA

It was taken for granted by the waiters that Sarne would share Tamsin's table. His place was set opposite hers at the window.

Sarne had called for her and whistled at her appearance. She wore a sleeveless, low-cut diagonally striped gown which followed her shape faithfully. The long zip fastener at the back had proved difficult to manage and she had panicked, but by twisting and reaching behind her, she had succeeded in sliding it to the top. Since she had no jewellery other than her mother's necklace, she wore that.

'*Another* dress?' he said, descending to the dining-room, his arm around her waist. She did not rise to his mocking surprise.

On their way to the table, they waved to the van Ruyters. During the meal, Sarne seemed preoccupied. When Luigi, the head waiter, attended them with the wine list, Sarne talked to him at length in Italian. It sounded as if Sarne was giving instructions as well as asking questions, to which Luigi replied, '*Si, si, signore,*' nodding as if to underline that he understood.

'Was that—work?' Tamsin ventured, when they were alone.

'Some of the delegates to the conference are staying here,' Sarne explained briefly. 'I had to make sure all the arrangements were in order.'

They were well into their first course when Sarne asked, 'What will you do for the next few days?'

Tamsin shook her head, feeling lost, as though Sarne, his companionship, support—and stirring presence, had already left her. But her words belied her uncertainty. 'I shall manage. I'll go on visits to places,' she said determinedly, 'perhaps go on the steamer again. Maybe even go south into Italy for a day.'

He smiled. 'All by yourself?'

'Why not?' she bristled. 'It's what I would have done, if—if you hadn't taken pity on me.'

'Pity?' he said. 'You were a gift from the skies! You fell straight into my lap—metaphorically, of course.' They laughed and he whispered, 'Into my arms.'

After dinner, they sat on a settee in the lounge. Tamsin read a book—at least, she hoped she gave the impression of doing so. Beside her, Sarne worked through a pile of papers. They seemed to be in many different languages. He was totally absorbed and it seemed to Tamsin that she had lost him already. But, as if in contradiction of her melancholy thoughts, Sarne looked at her, catching her wandering eyes. He smiled, reached out and held her right hand with his left. Her heart somersaulted, and she delighted in the physical contact with him. So he hadn't forgotten her!

'*Tu es très belle*,' he whispered. '*Tu comprends?*' Tamsin nodded mistily.

The receptionist came to stand in front of them. 'Miss Selby?' Tamsin nodded. 'You are wanted on the telephone.'

Tamsin frowned. Sarne looked up sharply. 'There must be some mistake,' Tamsin said. 'Sarne, I don't know anyone in Switzerland. Please,' she pleaded, 'could you sort it out?'

'This is a personal call from London, Miss Selby,' the receptionist said. 'A man called Mr—Mr Williams? Is that right? He is asking for you.'

'Mr Williams?' Tamsin frowned, then she smiled broadly. 'Of course, Mr William—I mean, Williams! It's all right, I understand now. Please, Sarne,' she detached her hand from his, 'will you look after my bag?' She hardly noticed his brief nod.

She followed the receptionist, keeping up with her brisk pace. Uncle William, she thought, Uncle William phoning her from London! 'I have been asked,' the receptionist said, 'that you should take the call in private in the office here.' She pointed to the room at the rear of the reception desk. 'Please make yourself at home.' She closed the door.

'Tamsin Selby here,' Tamsin said into the receiver.

'One moment,' said a brisk English voice. 'A personal call for you. Hold the line, please.'

Then, 'Tamsin, lass? It's your uncle here. Did you guess? Did you like my new name, Mr Williams? How are you, love? Enjoying yourself, eh? What's the weather doing? Sunshine all the way?'

Tamsin answered all his questions, telling him how she admired the country, thought the mountains were beautiful, the weather superb, the hotel excellent ...

'All's well, lass?' William asked. 'Got your list of complaints all made up for me when you come home?'

'Complaints?' She had almost forgotten the main reason for her being there—and at her uncle's expense! 'But there aren't any, Uncle. It's just great. Yes, everything! Lonely? Not at all. There's a man——' It was out before she had realised.

'A young man? She's met a young man! Is he English, lass? What's he like? Tall, dark and handsome?' Her uncle laughed loudly. 'He's got to be, to be good enough for our Tamsin!'

'Uncle, please, I—well, we——'

'She's gone all shy, Val. Here's your mother, love. Have a word, then with your dad.'

'Uncle, it must be costing a fortune!'

'Never mind that, lass. If I can't spend my money on my own, who can I spend it on? I'm handing over.'

'Mum? Oh, it's good to hear from you!'

'How are you, darling?' her mother asked. 'Are you eating well, dear? Keeping warm enough?' Tamsin laughed at the motherly concern. 'Are they looking after you properly? Did William say something about——?'

'He's just a friend, Mum,' Tamsin rushed in. 'He took pity on me because I looked so lonely, he said. There's nothing in it, honestly, Mum. We're—we're just friends. He's English—well, half. His mother's Italian–Swiss.'

They talked for a few more minutes, then Tamsin spoke to her father. She knew that he disliked phone calls and that he found it difficult to communicate verbally. She said, 'You'd love it here, Dad. It's so warm and sunny. You'll have to bring Mum one day.'

'It'll be a long time before you get me to go that distance, dear,' her father said, speaking with his customary slowness. Tamsin laughed. 'What's this about a——'

'It's nothing serious, Dad, honestly,' Tamsin protested, wishing she had not mentioned her acquaintance with Sarne Brand. Tamsin knew her father was anxious to get off the phone, so she asked, 'Is Uncle William still there?' William returned. 'Uncle,' Tamsin said, 'I do want to thank you for giving me this holiday. I won't stay too long——'

'Stay as long as you like, lass. I might pay a visit myself before long. Don't be surprised if someone calling himself Mr Bill Williams books in, will you? Well, it sounds better than William Williams, doesn't it? Better get off the phone and let others have a chance. 'Bye, my dear. Keep your eyes and ears open and don't tell anyone about me, will you? Look after yourself. Have a good time.'

Then they were gone. But they had left behind a light in Tamsin's eyes and a smile on her face which, she knew, would take a long time to fade. How could she hide it from Sarne? At reception she thanked the girl and lingered at the notice board, studying the pamphlets which had been pinned there advertising tours and visits to houses. There was a picture of a particularly intriguing villa which, it said, was open to the public at certain times.

The Villa Magnifico was near Morcote and coaches and steamers called there. She must go, she decided, in the week that Sarne was busy. After that week? No promises had been made by him that they would resume their crazy relationship. Yes, she told herself soberly, it was crazy, because there was no future in it, was there?

The thought dulled her happiness a little, but not

enough, it seemed, to hide from Sarne's perceptive eyes the exhilaration which still had hold of her.

'Well,' he asked, as she took her seat beside him, 'was the long-distance call worth the large amount of money it must have cost?'

'Oh yes,' she said eagerly, 'every penny——' She stopped, noticing the touch of sarcasm behind the question. 'A man –Mr Williams,' the receptionist had said. Tamsin, eyes wide, looked at Sarne. Was that what he was thinking? But how could she tell him, That was my uncle? She had been forbidden to tell anyone.

'I—I spoke to my mother and father,' she said. Would that persuade him it had not been a boy-friend who had called her?

Sarne frowned. 'Your parents, too? Quite a costly call. Whoever paid for it must have had a powerful motive.'

He looked at her as if expecting an answer, but she was silent. He returned to his work. 'Now I know,' he murmured, 'where the money comes from.' His hand did not stray to cover hers again.

She shook her head at his words, but it was true, wasn't it? How could she deny it? It was her uncle who was footing the bill all the time.

For a while, Tamsin sat quietly, gazing around yet not really seeing the house plants with large, spreading leaves, the standard lamps placed strategically near to chairs, the small paintings on the walls.

Thoughts of her long-distance conversation lingered, the excitement not yet completely extinguished. At home, life had been so simple. Why hadn't she stayed there? Why did she have to forsake that peace and quiet for the emotional turmoil into which she had been plunged from the moment she had arrived at this place?

It was all because of the man at her side, the man who, without even trying, had stirred in her a restlessness she could scarcely tolerate; who, with his kisses and his caresses, had aroused her to a longing she had never known before —a longing for a fulfilment which, because of the circumstances of their meeting, could never come to pass between them.

'Is something wrong?' The question forced her head towards him. 'You're fidgeting so much I can't concentrate.'

'I'm sorry, I'll——' She made to rise, but his hand came out.

'Like some coffee?' She nodded and he put aside his work, pocketed his pen and summoned a hovering waitress. He ordered a tray of coffee for two and looked at Tamsin. He smiled and the charm came sweeping back. A wave of pleasure rose, curled and descended, almost hurling her off balance.

They were friends again! He must have forgotten the phone call, or thrust it to the back of his mind, relegating it to the unimportant place to which it really belonged.

His arm came out, inviting her into it. 'Come nearer, Tamsin,' he said softly. 'You're too far away.'

She needed no further invitation. His arm closed about her so that there was not even room for a pocket of air between them. 'That's better,' he whispered, pressing his lips to the top of her head. She sighed, turning her face towards him. It was as if she was inviting a kiss. He did not wait to ask, his lips took hers, and Tamsin was glad they sat alone, that the other guests were dispersed throughout the spacious lounge.

When the waitress returned, setting out the cups, Tamsin leant forward to pour the coffee. Sarne did not remove his arm from her waist, it stayed there until she handed him his coffee. He lifted the cup in a mocking gesture. 'To the days we've spent together. May the memory of them remain untarnished in our minds.'

It was an odd toast and Tamsin's cup, on its way to her lips, faltered. Was he toasting the end of their friendship?

Was there nothing more to come? She drank, however, and forced a smile.

'What's wrong?' he asked for the second time. 'Your mouth has an upward tilt, but your eyes look sad. There must be a reason.'

Tamsin drank again and put down her cup. 'After—after the conference, Sarne, what will you do?'

'Stay on here. Why?'

She shrugged, as if it was of no consequence, but he saw through the action. He took a long drink and with a motion of the hand, asked for more coffee. Anxious to divert his thoughts, Tamsin obliged. He thanked her with a nod, stirred some sugar into the liquid and said thoughtfully,

'Are you asking me, in a roundabout way, if our—friendship will be resumed?'

She was cornered and could only nod. She poured herself a fresh cup of coffee and leant forward, away from his arm, to drink it. There was a tantalising silence, then he said,

'You realise that a—shall we say—relationship between a man and a woman can't stagnate? It can die away beyond resuscitation. Or it can progress, develop and deepen until, let's be frank, intimacy takes place?'

She coloured at his bluntness but nodded miserably.

'If you're aware of that,' he persisted, 'how can you expect our friendship to continue—unless, of course, you go into it with your eyes wide open, accepting everything that follows?'

'That "love affair" you said you'd like to have with me?' Her tone of voice sounded bitter.

His arm came round her again, pulling her against him. 'It's the way of things, *cara*,' he said softly. 'Before you decide, think carefully. Think, for instance, of—those you've left behind.'

'I've left no one behind,' she said irritably, 'except my family.'

'No? Not even a man called—Williams, wasn't it? Mr Williams? The man who paid so much for the chance to speak to you across many hundreds of miles? And gave you the opportunity to speak to your parents, too?'

'That was my——' If only she could tell the truth! If only she need have no secrets from this man ... But even if she told him the truth, clearing out of the way the suspicions he had of the existence of a boy-friend back home, what would it lead to? A mere love affair as he had implied, with no meaning, no lasting relationship, just an interlude to pass the time? That was all it would mean to Sarne Brand, whereas to her it would bring about a total commitment to him for the rest of her life. She would have given him everything of herself there was to give and, most important of all, her love.

'You haven't finished the sentence.' His voice, tinged with sarcasm, brought her back from torment.

'I'm tired, Sarne.' She rose. 'Do you mind if I go up?'

'Not at all.' He gathered his papers. There was no need, she told him hastily, for him to accompany her ... He ignored the statement.

In the lift, he stared at the floor. Tamsin closed her eyes. At her door, she found the key, turned it and said, 'Thanks for coming with me, Sarne. Now you can get on with your work uninterrupted.' She smiled and started to close the door, but his shoulder stopped her.

'Aren't you going to offer me a drink?' She frowned, puzzled. 'You owe me one, don't you? From your mini-bar?'

'Oh, I—I forgot! Of—of course I do. Yes, do come in. How silly of me!'

'You're fluttering,' he grinned. 'A drink, *cara*. That's why I came in—wasn't it?'

Tamsin heard the innuendo in the misleadingly soft voice and hurriedly opened the door of the refrigerated mini-bar where the miniature bottles were stored. She had no wish to prolong the agony of having him there, yet knowing that tomorrow would bring with it an end to their friendship.

The mini-bar was next to the bedside table and Tamsin sat on the bed and read the list of contents which were fixed to the door of the mini-bar.

'Sarne, I'm hopeless at this,' she said. 'Would you like to come and choose?'

He joined her, sitting on the bed beside her, and consulted the list. 'It's the same as mine. Gin for me,' he selected a small bottle and then took another. 'And tonic water. What about you?'

'Nothing, thanks.'

'Oh, come on now, I refuse to drink alone. Dubonnet,' he held up a small dark green bottle, 'is that what you'd like?'

She nodded, giving in. Give in, she thought as she watched him the bottles and pour the drinks, wasn't that what she was always doing where this man was concerned? What troubled her most was how long she would go on doing so and where, in their relationship, she would call a halt.

'Drink,' he said, handing her a glass containing the deep red liquid, 'drink and enjoy it. Who knows,' he savoured the taste of the contents of his glass, 'when we shall drink together, do anything together, again?' His half-smile and raised eyebrows called for an answer from her, as if it were entirely for her to decide on their future friendship. But she was silent, sipping her drink.

He swallowed the last few drops from his glass, put it down and wandered to the window. For some time he stood there, staring out. Now and then Tamsin looked at him, wondering whether or not to speak. Her glass clinked against the table top of the mini-bar, then she stood uncertainly in the middle of the room.

'Tamsin?'

'Yes?'

His hand came out although his face remained averted.

Put your hand in mine, the gesture said. It was an invitation she accepted without reserve. She crossed to the window and clasped his hand, but it seemed he was not content with that. His arm lifted to her shoulders and he pulled her close.

Together they gazed at the moonlit mountains, at the silver path thrown across the waters of the lake. As he said, who was to know when they would do anything together again? Her arm lifted, tentatively, then with resolution to his waist.

By such a movement, she knew she had told him that she had given in. He had won. If he wished to take it as a signal that she wanted their relationship to continue, to develop, to lead to the ultimate conclusion, she was telling him silently that he could do so. She asked herself, Why not make the short time that was left before they had to part a time to remember, to relish, to store in the memory and recall with a rush of warmth when the ice-cold future closed in?

His head came round and there was an expression in his eyes that sent a kind of liquid fire leaping through her veins. He caught her by the shoulders and closed the gap between them.

'Is this your answer?' he asked, and she was too intoxicated by the touch, the magnetism of him to notice the hardness that had crept into his voice. 'That, despite all other claims on your affections and your faithfulness, in the face of any other emotional attachment there may be in your life, you're telling me "I'm yours if you want me"? My word,' there was no overlooking the edge, the hint of ruthlessness now, 'I need no more encouragement than that!'

Too late she realised his meaning, that, in spite of the fact that there was, or so he thought, another man in her life, she was giving him, as he had said when he had kissed her during the storm, 'no signal at red, no sign telling him to stop'.

She was in his arms and his mouth was on hers, pressing her down, down until she was forced to cling to him. He swung her upright and the kiss, although still ruthless, became more intimate, coaxing from her at first an unwilling, then a rapturous, response and surrender.

His fingers found the long zip at the back of her dress, sliding it down until the gown fell from her shoulders. His hands slipped inside, finding the breasts beneath, moulding them, stroking, exciting her senses beyond endurance. As she began to submit to his physical domination of her body, so her mind began to yield, too.

There was no doubt that he knew by now that he had won. There was also no doubt, by the way he fondled her, running his palms over her shape, prising her lips wide and kissing her with a force and a familiarity that had her gasping for breath, that there was no tenderness in his lovemaking. He was subtly, sickeningly, insulting her.

'I want you,' he said thickly, 'and I'm going to take you. Let's make ourselves comfortable, my sweet. Where better than the bed?'

As he urged her towards it, the meaning of his words slowly penetrated the mists that had gathered around her brain.

'No,' she muttered, trying to fight his greater strength, 'no.' They had reached the bed. 'No!' she cried, her thoughts breaking free at last from the spell he had imposed on them. 'I told you,' her voice rose as he began to force her down, 'it's not my way. For me there's got to be love before—before I'd let a man——'

She broke off in despair. She was making no impression. His hand was at her throat and he was cursing the high neck of her dress. 'There's no love in you,' she cried, 'not even any compassion. There's only lust and a wish for some reason to hurt me and give me pain.'

His body, pressing her down on to the bed, was still. His head came up and she could see the twin fires of anger which still blazed in his eyes. Her voice fell to a whisper and she pleaded, although with small hope of succeeding, 'Sarne, please, *please* let me go.'

It seemed that she had at last got through to his humanity if not his kindliness. He shifted from her and, freed of his weight, she lay still, her head turned to one side. She was pale, exhausted—and despairing. When she opened her eyes, there was no mistaking the scorn with which he regarded her. She swung her legs to the floor and rose to face him.

He took some money from a pocket and held out the notes. She looked at him, puzzled. 'For the drinks,' he said curtly.

She shook her head. 'You wouldn't let me pay for mine when I came to your room.'

'Then take it in payment,' he looked her over evaluatingly and she grew conscious of her dishevelled state, the way her dress had fallen from her shoulders, 'for—other things.'

His eyes narrowed speculatingly. He looked at her breasts still covered by the scant lace bra she was wearing. Slowly, holding her eyes all the time, he folded the notes and thrust them deep into the cleft.

'I hope it's enough, *signorina*,' he murmured silkily. 'I always pay a woman well, especially one who has particularly pleased me. Next time,' his smile was thin and humourless, 'if you please me more, I'll pay you more.'

She swayed, feeling faint, but his look merely hardened. He turned from her, picked up the pile of papers he had brought with him and left her.

Tamsin watched him go, then sank on to the bed, head in hands. She felt sick, distraught and humiliated beyond belief.

CHAPTER SIX

NEXT day, a crowd of new guests arrived. Since they neither dressed nor talked like tourists, Tamsin concluded that they were delegates to the international conference at which Sarne was engaged to act as interpreter.

She did not see Sarne until the evening. Having no enthusiasm to do anything else, she had swum lethargically in the morning and sunbathed, talking now and then to the Dutch couple. They were there, they told her, for another week.

All day Tamsin had half hoped, half dreaded, that she would see Sarne. In the afternoon, she had sat on a swing seat under the trees and watched the comings and goings, trying in vain to tear her mind from the man who had left her so brutally to her misery the evening before. As people met and introductions were made, she heard the words 'Professor' and *'Professeur'* and 'Doctor', applied to women as well as to men.

There were, she decided, swinging to and fro a little forlornly, many cultured and highly educated people visiting the town, people who would regard a newly-qualified, unemployed primary schoolteacher like herself with something approaching condescension, if not a touch of disdain.

She sighed and looked at her watch. It was almost time for dinner. She decided to go upstairs and change, although she felt reluctant to take much care with her appearance. Now Sarne had withdrawn his friendship, it did not matter what she looked like.

In the lounge there was a crowd of people, as indeed there had been all day. The volume of noise had increased, however, and the variety of languages had become even more bewildering. As Tamsin pushed her way to the foot of the stairs, a man was coming down it, a tall, brown-eyed man with a proud bearing. The sight of him had Tamsin's heart beating frenziedly.

'Ah,' said a man's voice from the crowd, 'Professor Brand, how good to see you!'

Sarne Brand swept past the white-faced, wide-eyed girl at the foot of the stairs as if she did not exist. His full, sensitive lips were curved into a smile, his hand outstretched in greeting. It was clasped by the hand of the speaker.

Slowly Tamsin climbed the stairs. At the bend she turned, looking down on the crowd. 'Sarne,' she heard a woman's voice say, 'how good to see you! It will be wonderful working with you again.'

Tamsin searched for the woman. It was not difficult finding her because Sarne was with her, grasping her hand and kissing her cheek.

'Nona,' his voice carried above the chatter, 'I hoped you would come. Delightful to see you here.' Then his attention was claimed by others and Tamsin went miserably on her way.

From her balcony she gazed at the swimming pool. Around it stood empty chairs and tables which had been tidied by the hotel staff. The sky was darkening and in the underwater lights that had been switched on, she could see a spattering of raindrops. So the weather had changed to suit her mood.

Dully she thought, Professor—*Professor* Brand! So that was what he was! It explained so many puzzling things—his prolonged vacation, his expensive car, his air of detachment, the reserve she had stumbled on now and then so disconcertingly during their short but never-to-be-forgotten acquaintance.

Why hadn't he told her? But he had been under no obligation to do so. She had told him nothing about herself. And hadn't they agreed—no past, no future? Now she understood why. He had had no wish to become embarrassingly involved with a girl who was merely passing through his life. What had she been to him, after all, but a female to kiss and, with any luck, use for the indulgence of his desires?

And she had allowed herself to be taken in by him, to be flattered, to let her emotions be ensnared—to fall deeply in love with the man! She could have cried with mortification, anger and despair.

Dispiritedly Tamsin took a shower, dressed in a simply-styled floral summer dress and ran a comb through her clustering curls. She wished she had brought some jeans and shirts with her. Tonight she would have worn them and defied convention. At least she would have looked different from those high-powered intellectuals down there with whom Sarne Brand was now mixing—his equal in education, intelligence and achievement.

How he would laugh, she thought bitterly, if she had told him she was an unemployed schoolteacher. From his pinnacle of learning he would regard her as of less importance than a pin to a dressmaker. She wondered as she closed her door and made for the stairs what the subject was in which he held his professorship.

At dinner, Sarne sat among the delegates. He seemed, even then, to be busy interpreting so that the people around him could converse. Opposite him, at the long table the management had provided to accommodate the guests, sat the woman who had greeted him so warmly.

Had she enjoyed the feel of his lips as they had touched her cheek? Tamsin wondered sourly. Had the woman experienced Sarne Brand's passion, as she, Tamsin, had done? Had he charmed *her*, smiled his irresistible 'Italian' smile, looked at her with his warm, brown 'Italian' eyes?

Maybe, Tamsin reflected, staring out of the window, he did not know the woman well enough to have become so intimate with her. But, she thought with dismay, how long has Sarne known me? Four or five days? Yet it had not prevented their friendship from developing so fast that he had felt entitled to make ardent love to her!

Tamsin stole a glance at the woman. Yes, she was about Sarne's age, attractive in a cool fashion, self-assured, dark-haired, perfectly groomed. By the way she was alternately listening to people and then speaking, as Sarne was doing, it seemed that she, too, was an interpreter, which meant that she was as good at speaking other languages as Sarne himself.

Repeatedly Tamsin found her eyes drawn to Sarne. She could not help it. Once he caught her eye. He did not smile, but merely looked back at her coldly and she withdrew her gaze with haste and embarrassment. Now he would guess at her thoughts, that she was missing his company and feeling alone again. If he did, he showed no sign. It was as though he had mentally shrugged his shoulders and was thinking, 'Let her get on with it. She's brought it on herself.'

After dinner, the clouds massed darkly over the mountains, making the lake look black and menacing. Tamsin, gazing out of her window, knew that before long it would rain. She found a book and a magazine and took them downstairs to the hotel lounge.

To her dismay, it seemed as though the whole place was filled to capacity. The lounge was full of people. She had reckoned without the fact that, in such unpalatable weather, everyone would remain in the hotel instead of walking about the windswept town.

With anxious eyes she searched for an unoccupied seat, discovering one at last half-hidden in a corner. It was not difficult to find Sarne. His height brought him above most of the other men even if some strange sort of instinct had not drawn her eyes towards him.

Now she knew his status in life, Tamsin did not wonder at the quality of his clothes, the excellent taste in which he could indulge. At his side, gazing up at him, was the woman he had called Nona. There was no doubting the admiration in her eyes as she listened raptly to what he was saying.

Did he admire her, Tamsin wondered, with the same intensity? Her long black dress was clinging and a triple row of pearls rested on the woman's slender neck. Would he, Tamsin wondered again, making for the solitary chair before someone else occupied it, accuse the woman at his side of following him about 'like a pet dog its beloved master'? as he had accused her the day after she had arrived? Would he accuse the woman called Nona of fastening on to him, of watching for him and inviting him with her eyes to sit beside him, as Tamsin recalled he had done to her?

She shrank into her corner, away from the laughter and the loud voices she could not understand and tried to escape into her book. But if anyone had been interested enough to watch her, they would have seen her attention wander frequently from the printed pages. They would have noticed how her eyes kept moving over the people grouped around the long, low tables or who sat in ever-widening circles as friends and acquaintances joined them. And they would have sensed how lonely she felt as she searched for familiar faces—even perhaps one familiar face amongst those strangers.

'Tamsin?' She almost jumped out of her chair at the nearness of the voice, knowing who the person was by the way he said her name.

She looked up into two brown eyes, eyes that were no longer warm. They were cool and inscrutable and remote. So this was the 'English' side of him, the side he had warned her to 'steer clear of' this holiday.

'There's no need,' Sarne said, hands in his pockets, 'for you to hide yourself in a corner. I'm perfectly willing to introduce you to some of the people attending the conference. I'll interpret where necessary.'

Tamsin did not answer at once. She would have loved to

have gone with him, to have talked to these newcomers, who seemed so full of laughter and vitality. But as his equal, as his friend and not merely because he had taken pity on her —once again—in her lonely state. She could never, she told herself, biting her lip and looking at the assembled company, be this man's equal and certainly not his friend.

Her eyes found his again and she tried to recall how they had looked the two or three days they had spent together. They had filled her with delight, with an excitement that had plunged her nervous system into a state of chaos. In those few days she had known only that she had wanted him to remain at her side for the rest of her holiday—and, came a whisper, of her life!

Now they were the eyes of a stranger and she shrank from their coldness.

'No, thank you, *Professor* Brand,' a sudden spurt of anger made her emphasise the word, 'it would be wasted effort on your part. There would be no point in introducing me to people who, literally as well as metaphorically, didn't speak my language. I've got nothing in common with such people,' her hand indicated the crowd around them, 'with people of culture and scientific achievement, and who hold doctorates and *professorships*.'

'That was quite a speech.' His mocking smile goaded her.

'In fact,' she whispered furiously, 'I don't know how you managed to tolerate my company for the past week. After all, I'm only an ignorant female who does nothing to earn her living, yet can afford to spend weeks at a time at a luxury hotel like this. All, of course, paid for by a rich boyfriend who's got so much money he can afford to put an expensive call through to her from London.'

His hands went to his hips and rested there. It was a slightly belligerent attitude that challenged. 'All right, Miss Selby,' she winced at his formality, but hadn't she become formal towards him? 'if it wasn't a rich boy-friend, who was it?'

She had been sworn to silence. She could not give her uncle away.

'You see, you don't answer. Which means it must be true.'

It's *not* true, she was about to say, but closed her lips tightly. He wouldn't believe her, so what was the use?

She stood, which brought her face dauntingly near his. He smiled—with his lips. His eyes remained cold. Was he remembering the last time he had kissed her? And how he had *paid* her—for her favours? He did not move to let her pass and near as she was to him, she felt the pulling power of his body, the invisible tentacles that reached out from him to her, ensnaring her all over again and from which it was a physical effort to disentangle herself.

He smiled, appearing to know the internal struggle she was experiencing. But he did not move.

'Please, Professor Brand,' her voice faltered, 'let me go past.'

'Why should I?' His smile had gone and she shook her head helplessly. 'Drop the formality,' he said curtly.

'Please, Sarne,' she whispered, and he moved aside.

Upstairs she pulled on a coat and tied a silk scarf around her head. Then she ran down the stairs, made her way round the groups of people and opened the glass entrance door. Outside, the wind blew and in the light from the coloured lamps which were strung from tree to tree, she could see drops of falling rain. But she pushed her hands into her pockets, took a breath—

'Now where are you going?' The same voice, but this time a hand on her shoulder detained her.

Irritably she shook herself free of it. 'Out,' she said, 'out, anywhere. For a walk, it doesn't matter where.'

'It's raining.'

'I can see that for myself, thanks. Anyway,' she turned

115

on him and the floodlights which funnelled their beams on to the hotel exterior shone full on Sarne's face, 'why should you trouble yourself about me? I'm not your responsibility.'

The light cast shadows around his eyes and mouth, turning him into even more of a stranger. And she thought she had come to know him during the few days they had spent together!

'You might get lost.'

'If I do,' she retorted, 'nothing would make you happier, would it? I'd be off your back, then. There'd be no pest of a "little dog" following you about!' She dashed down the steps and escaped along the drive to meet the main road. A glance over her shoulder told her he had not followed.

She walked for some time beside the lake, watching the reflected lights staining the water with rippling colour. Now and then a ferry boat approached the jetty, emerging from the darkness, its interior lighting splashing out on to the lake. A group of white swans glided by. In spite of the rain there were people walking as she was doing, collars up, scarves or umbrellas over their heads.

When she returned to the hotel and climbed the steps, she remembered the day of her arrival there. At the top of the steps had stood a man, dark-haired, dark-eyed, leaning indolently against the door. It was a man she would remember all her life. She wouldn't see him again, she told herself, because he had gone for ever.

Across the room was a man resembling him facially, nothing more. That man was looking at her and the expression on his face told her he had been waiting for her return. Now she was there, she held no more interest for him because he turned his back. Obviously he had felt some responsibility for her in her absence, but now his responsibility had ended.

Tamsin could have cried. Even though Sarne Brand had turned into the 'Englishman' he had warned her against, she couldn't stop loving him. Deep inside that 'English' coolness was an ardent lover, a laughing, warm-eyed, demanding man who, one day, would tell some fortunate woman that he loved her. By then she, Tamsin, would have gone out of his life and he would probably have difficulty in recalling her name, let alone what she looked like.

The following morning the weather had improved and the sun shone with its former intensity. After breakfast, there was an exodus from the hotel as the delegates went off in their cars and taxis to the conference hall.

Most of them had gone by the time Tamsin found her way to the terrace where breakfast was being served. There was no sign of Sarne or of the woman called Nona. Tamsin helped herself to the minimum of food. She simply was not hungry.

It was a day for relaxing and Tamsin, putting on her swimsuit, and with a towel round her shoulders, ran through the hotel and out to the pool. She put her belongings on a chair and found that the pool, since it was early, was almost empty. Whatever her feelings, however depressed she might feel about other events, it was good to plunge into the water and strike out from one end to the other. After a while she emerged and ran, dripping, across the paving stones to her chair, towelling herself to tingling dryness.

Mr and Mrs van Ruyter came down the steps and joined her, occupying the chairs next to hers. They exchanged pleasantries and settled themselves, Mrs van Ruyter saying that she loved the sunshine so much they would probably sit there all day.

'The hotel is full to bursting point,' Mrs van Ruyter said. 'This conference is keeping Mr Brand busy.'

'And away from you,' said Mr van Ruyter with a sympathetic smile. 'It's a pity. But never mind, when it's over, he will have time to accompany you again. You are so pretty, I'm sure he can hardly wait for the week to go!'

Tamsin blushed and they laughed at her embarrassment.

'It's true what my husband says,' Mrs van Ruyter commented. 'In fact, we were surprised that you are here alone. The young men in England must be very slow.'

They laughed again and this time Tamsin joined them.

'It was good of Mr Brand to interrupt his holiday and help out the organisers of the conference,' Mr van Ruyter said. 'It seems he's filling in for two absent interpreters. He told us the work is a great strain.'

Tamsin frowned. 'In what way? I should have thought that for someone as expert at languages as he seems to be, it would be easy.'

'Not at all. It is what is called instant interpretation, a split-second timing where the translation is almost immediate. The interpreter wears headphones, as do the people at the receiving end, and no sooner has the speaker spoken his words than the interpreter is translating them in his mind and speaking that translation into a microphone to the listeners. In fact, it is such a strain that normally interpreters are only allowed to work for a certain specified length of time. Then they must rest, before they start again.'

'Mr Brand told us that it requires great concentration,' his wife added. 'It must be very exhausting.'

It seemed that Sarne Brand had spoken at length to Mr and Mrs van Ruyter about his work, but nothing at all to the girl he had befriended. Maybe, she thought, he considered that her intelligence was not good enough to understand the situation.

'Does—does Mr Brand have a job?' Tamsin asked, wondering if they knew any more about him. 'I heard them call him "Professor Brand" and——'

'Oh, but of course,' Mr van Ruyter said. 'He is here on vacation, his long vacation. He is professor of modern languages at a university in—how do you English call it—the middle lands of England?'

For a moment Tamsin was puzzled, then she laughed.

'Oh, you mean the Midlands. It's what we call the area around Birmingham and Coventry and so on. So,' she frowned, 'that's what he is—a university professor.'

'I'm not surprised you're surprised,' Mr van Ruyter said, smiling. 'He doesn't look in the least like a university don, does he? They get younger and younger these days.'

'He's so good-looking,' Mrs van Ruyter sighed. 'Oh, to be a pretty young girl like you who catches his eye!'

His eye but not his heart, Tamsin thought bitterly.

That afternoon, she wandered round the shops buying presents for her parents and friends. It was not that she intended to leave for home yet, but since the shops were some distance from the hotel, she thought that while she was in the town, she might as well buy a few gifts.

Tamsin found herself lingering in front of some of the many jewellers' shops, admiring the gold and silver and the precious stones. Her uncle had given her so much money she knew she would have had sufficient to buy at least one item of jewelllery for herself but felt it would be wrong to do so. If she spent too much, it would take her years to repay the money.

Next day was Sunday, but the conference continued, although the morning session began later than the day before.

As Tamsin wandered down the drive, she noticed that Sarne's car was still parked, which meant that he was probably still on the hotel premises. But he was nearer to her than she had thought.

'Tamsin?' He was coming along behind her, dressed with his usual care, his diagonally striped tie flying in the breeze. 'Can I give you a lift? Are you going into the town?'

'No, thank you,' she said, hoping she sounded offhanded. She would not tell him where she was going, that she was merely intending to walk along the lakeside. If she did, he would know that she had no plans and from this he would deduce, accurately, that she was lonely. And it had been her loneliness, hadn't it, that had drawn him to her side in the first place? He had offered his company out of pity, not interest or a desire to get to know her better.

He shrugged and unlocked his car. He drove past her, but had to wait at the entrance before joining the main road, until there was a gap in the traffic.

So Tamsin drew level with him, strolling past as if she had not a care in the world. A prolonged wolf whistle, echoed by another, had her head spinning round. Just outside the hotel entrance there were two young men, rucksacks on the ground beside them. Their thumbs were pointing in the direction in which they wished to go. They were dressed in jeans and jackets and they wore walking boots on their feet. On their faces were broad grins.

If Sarne had not been sitting there, if his head had not come round at the whistles as hers had done—his with irritation, hers with a ripple of pleasure at the flattery—she would have ignored the two young men and passed them as though they had not existed. But perversely, and with a desire for revenge—why should he have his woman called Nona and she have no one?—she turned her most charming smile on the two young men. The whistles were repeated, but louder this time and even more long drawn out.

'Hi, there,' one of them called to Tamsin. '*Sprechen Sie Deutsch, Fräulein?*'

'*Nein*,' she replied, laughing, 'only English.'

'Going our way?' said the other, his grin growing wider.

There must have been a gap in the traffic at last because Sarne's car shot forward dangerously fast and was swallowed up in the never-ending stream of vehicles.

Tamsin forgot about the young men as she walked by the lakeside, but when she returned, they were still there. One was sitting on the ground, his back against the wall of the hotel, while the other continued to try and persuade a car driver to stop and give them a lift.

They looked so miserable, Tamsin asked sympathetically, 'No luck?'

They shook their heads. 'Been here over an hour. At this rate, we'll have to spend the night here.'

She laughed and went on her way. The young men were visible from her balcony and as she watched them, she hoped for their sakes that they succeeded in their efforts soon. It was far too hot to have to sit in the sun unprotected for such a long time.

They were still there when she returned to her room after lunch. Now she really felt sorry for them. They were both seated on the ground and seemed to be eating sandwiches and drinking from cans. Even from that distance she could discern a droop about their shoulders which revealed how discouraged they had grown.

Tamsin relaxed on the balcony, closing her eyes simply for the pleasure of opening them again and seeing the view which greeted her every time—the steeply sloping sides of Monte Brè with its hotels and houses and red-roofed villas glinting in the sunshine. The mountains in the distance towered one above the other while great white cloud formations hovered over them.

Down in the driveway there were voices in many languages and the slamming of car doors. Tamsin leaned over the balcony parapet and saw that the voices belonged to the conference delegates. The day's session, having begun late, must also have ended early, probably because it was a Sunday. Which meant, and her heart leapt, that Sarne would be returning soon, too.

'Hi, there!' Tamsin peered down the slope of the drive, but the two young men had gone. Instead, they were just outside the hotel and stood gazing up at her.

'Come down, oh, Juliet, to your Romeo,' said the other, his hand on his heart.

Their rucksacks were on their backs and one had his foot on the lowest step as though they intended entering the hotel. What were they doing? she thought, dismayed. One of them had said, 'At this rate, we'll have to spend the night here.' At the time, Tamsin had thought they were joking, but it seemed not.

Did they know, she wondered, how expensive the hotel was to stay at? She was certain that they did not have sufficient money between them to pay for a night's stay for one, let alone two.

'Wait a moment!' she called, and rushed from her room, down the curved marble staircase to find them in the entrance foyer.

'Hi, Juliet,' one of them said. 'Romeo at your service.'

'Where's the red carpet?' said the other.

'You can't stay here,' Tamsin told them breathlessly.

'Why not?' one of them asked, looking round. 'It's a free country.' He hesitated. 'Isn't it? I always thought Switzerland was, anyway.'

Tamsin's colour heightened as she sought for words to tell them, without hurting their feelings, just why they couldn't stay there. Sarne burst in through the swing doors and Tamsin had to restrain herself from running to him for help. But one look at his scowling face was enough to push that idea from her mind.

He looked at her, then he looked at the young men. Tamsin knew from his expression in just which category he was placing them—and herself for appearing so friendly with perfect strangers. In defiance, she turned her back on him. She heard him pass and go up the stairs.

'This hotel,' she explained, 'it's—well, it's an expensive place to stay in.'

'That's obvious,' said the one who had called himself Romeo. He took a breath. 'The air is redolent with affluence.'

'He can't help it,' said the other, nudging his friend, who proceeded to "collapse" from the blow, 'he speaks like that naturally. He means the place smells of money.'

'Well,' Tamsin said agitatedly, 'you see what I mean.'

'It's all right,' said "Romeo", 'we're loaded, too. At least,

I am.' Giving his friend a mock-contemptuous look, 'He's just a hanger-on.'

'What he means,' said his friend, 'is that his father owns a chain of highly respectable department stores across Britain. We're students and we both attend the same university.'

'I decided to see how the other half lives,' "Romeo" said, 'and he decided to come with me. We're both hostelling our way across Europe.'

'Go on,' said his friend to Tamsin, 'tell us this isn't a youth hostel.'

'I did hear,' Tamsin said, laughing at the young man's banter, 'that there's a youth hostel just outside Lugano.'

'Ah,' said Romeo, shifting his rucksack from his shoulders and lowering it to the ground, 'we've just come from there, and we don't want to go back because, well——' he grinned, 'Juliet's not there, is she?'

Tamsin coloured. 'I'm not sure what you mean.'

'Tell her, Douglas,' Romeo said.

'Well, as Roger says,' said Douglas, 'you—Juliet—are here, not there. So, being unable to persuade a single driver to take us on to the next stopping place and fancying a night or two spent in luxurious surroundings——'

'You missed out the most important part,' said Roger. 'Liking the look of the occupants—well,' he grinned, too, 'one of the occupants of the hotel——'

'He,' said Douglas, taking up the story, 'offered to treat me to said one or two nights of luxury living because he took my girl-friend away from me at college.'

'Excuse me,' said a frigid voice behind them.

'Oh—oh, sorry,' the young men said, and shifted their large rucksacks from Sarne Brand's path. 'We're taking up too much room.'

Sarne circled round them and stood at the reception desk as if awaiting attention. There was one girl on duty and she was already dealing with a guest's query.

'As we were saying,' said Roger, 'I've got his girl-friend, not because I took her from him but because she gave me the sign.' To Tamsin: 'It's always the girl who gives the sign.'

Tamsin laughed helplessly, regardless of the scathing look directed at her by the man waiting impatiently at the desk. 'Is it? I don't think that's——'

'Oh, it's true all right. When a man sees that sign, he——'

'Anyway,' said Douglas, 'he said——' he nudged his friend, 'if we—well, made your acquaintance, you might give *me* the "sign" and what do you know? I've got myself another girl-friend. Come on, Roger, you're the one with the money. Let's book ourselves in.'

They moved to stand at reception. The girl turned to Sarne Brand, who said, 'I would like to book a table for two tonight, instead of dining with the delegation. For myself and Miss Hampton.'

'Yes, of course, sir,' the girl said.

So, Tamsin thought, he's dining with her alone tonight. Sick at heart, she kept her eyes down as he left. No wonder he wanted to bring his acquaintance with Tamsin Selby to an end, knowing that a woman friend of his was coming to stay at the hotel.

Yes, the receptionist told Roger, there was a double room free—on the third floor. 'Room three hundred and three,' she said.

With a shock, Tamsin remembered that Sarne's room number was three hundred, so Roger and Douglas would be only three rooms away from him. Then she thought, what did it matter? She wouldn't be visiting them, would she?

Tamsin made her way down to dinner. She had chosen a simple dress in different shades of pink and had slipped into white sandals. She knew she would be no match for the beautiful Miss Nona Hampton, but where Sarne's lady friend was concerned, she knew also that she was fighting a hopeless battle.

As soon as Tamsin entered the dining-room, she saw Sarne and his guest. The woman's chin rested on her clasped hands and she was gazing at Sarne over the small bowl of flowers. Were those warm brown male eyes looking at her as, only days—or was it weeks?—ago, they had gazed at Tamsin Selby?

Tamsin had to pass their table and as she did so, Sarne's eyes flicked up to her. Of their own accord, hers met his. His glance told her nothing, but how much did hers give away to him? At that moment she felt so miserable some of it was sure to have got through to her eyes.

'Hey, Juliet,' a voice called in a stage whisper, 'come and join us!'

Tamsin, having passed Sarne's table, saw the two young men. 'I've got a table of my own,' she protested weakly. 'It might confuse the waiters if——'

'*Signorina*,' Luigi hovered, 'if you wish to change your table, please, it is no trouble.' So Tamsin dined with Roger and Douglas.

'You're looking surprisingly tidy,' she told them, smiling. 'And my name's Tamsin Selby, not Juliet.'

'Hi, Tamsin,' they said. 'We've made full use of the first-class facilities. We've showered, shaved, found a comb and combed our hair——'

'All for you,' said Douglas. 'Roger even went out and bought us a tie each, just so that we wouldn't let you down.'

Tamsin was touched. 'I don't know why,' she said.

'You don't? Looked in a mirror lately?' asked Douglas. 'You're great, you've got something others haven't got. You got a boy-friend?'

'Yes and no.' Two sets of eyebrows shot up. 'Well,' Tamsin qualified, 'maybe two or three.'

Douglas mopped his brow. 'For a minute, I thought I had a rival.'

They chatted throughout the meal and somehow Tamsin managed to keep her mind, and her eyes, off Sarne Brand and his companion in another part of the dining-room.

Making 'I've eaten too much' gestures, Douglas said, 'Let's move. Okay, Roger?'

They spent the evening in the bar. Looking about her, Tamsin remembered with pain when Sarne had taken her there. She saw with a lurch of the heart that he was there again, but this time with another woman at his side. They were seated so that, if she looked carefully out of the corner of her eyes, Tamsin could see them. Which was how she knew that, now and then, Sarne would turn his head and glance narrowly at the laughing group a few tables distant from him.

'You a student, too?' Roger asked, lifting his tankard of beer. Tamsin shook her head. 'What's your job, then?'

Tamsin took a sip of the sherry her companions had insisted on buying her. 'Haven't got one.'

'Unemployed?' Douglas asked. Tamsin nodded and Douglas made a sympathetic face. 'How come?'

'I've just qualified as a primary schoolteacher. Nobody wants me on their staff so, along with thousands of others, I've joined the queue for teaching jobs.'

'And yet you can afford to come to a place like this for your vacation?'

Douglas's question confused her. Not even to these two very pleasant young men could she tell the truth. Even if they discussed it when they were alone in their room, someone might overhear. Anyway, they would get the wrong impression of her—that she came of a wealthy family. One member of her family was wealthy, of course, but it gave her no pleasure always to have to confess that her mother and father were the poor relations.

'Pure chance,' she said, evading the question. 'Special circumstances.'

Her companions waited for more, but when it did not

come, Roger said, 'The lady's not willing to tell. Anyway, it's none of our business.'

'Too true,' said Douglas with a sigh. 'Tamsin,' he murmured behind his hand, 'there's a dark Italian-looking type a couple of tables away who can't keep his eyes off you. Keeps looking at us as though we're planning a crime and you're going to be our victim. Happen to know him?'

'Yes,' said Tamsin shortly. 'He's staying here. He's a university professor.'

'Well now, who'd have guessed?' said Roger. 'I like his taste in females. Very smooth, very tasty.'

'I don't,' said Douglas. 'I prefer Juliet—I mean Tamsin.' They laughed and Sarne's eyes swung towards them. 'So he's a prof. Well, well. They don't come like that often, even these days. They're usually bearded or bespectacled——'

'Or bald,' finished Roger, and they laughed again. 'What's his subject? Science, like us?'

'No, he's professor of modern languages at a university in the Midlands. I got the information secondhand. He didn't tell me.'

'Do I detect,' said Roger, 'a note of pique? Are you a dark horse, Tamsin? Do you know the gentleman better than we think?'

Tamsin coloured. 'We—we did get friendly. We had a row.'

'Ah—ah!' It was a long-drawn-out sound from Roger. 'Now I see. You're too late, Douglas, my friend. The lady's not heartwhole.'

Douglas thumped his knee. 'Darn it! But she said they had a row, which meant it's all off. Right, Tamsin?'

Tamsin, lifting her shoulders, pushed her empty glass around with lifeless fingers.

'Hey, let's do the lady a good turn, Douglas,' said Roger. 'Let's make the man jealous. Let's give him something to think about. That'll take his mind off his current girlfriend!'

'What's the use?' said Tamsin despondently. 'How can I compete with her? She's not only good to look at, she's a languages expert, too. She's an interpreter, like he is, at this international convention they're holding in the town.'

Nevertheless Tamsin's companions shifted nearer. Douglas put his arm round her waist and Roger captured her shoulders. Douglas pulled her face round and kissed her on the lips, while Roger ruffled her hair. Tamsin protested indignantly at such behaviour, but they were not deterred.

'It's working,' Roger muttered. 'He's looking at us as though he'd love to have us thrown out by the management.'

Tamsin stole a glance at Sarne and winced at what she saw. The contempt in his eyes was intended, she knew, for her alone. In his opinion, it was her brazen encouragement which gave rise to the unruly and uninhibited behaviour of her two companions.

'Come on,' said Douglas, 'respond. Let him think you're enjoying yourself. At least it's keeping his mind off the woman he's with.'

Tamsin laughed. They were so good-natured and they were doing their best for her.

Moments later, Sarne rose, inviting his guest to follow. They left the bar without a backward glance.

'There now,' said Roger, 'that should have helped make him jealous.'

But Tamsin knew it was anger, not jealousy which had precipitated Sarne's sudden departure.

Next day, she was invited by the two young men to join them in a coach drive which would take them across the frontier into Italy. 'It includes a trip across Lake Como to Bellagio,' Douglas told her.

She asked herself, Why should I sit around longing for the sight of a man to whom I mean nothing? Hadn't he found himself, without any scruples, another woman to take her place?

Tamsin accepted the invitation, insisting on paying her own way, despite the 'hoards of money' of which Roger boasted. The weather had turned colder and it rained as they drove through the countryside. Before crossing the border into Italy, they were asked to produce their passports and were given immediate clearance.

The view they would have seen from the ferry boat as it took them across Lake Como was shrouded in a rain-soaked mist and they stood on deck shivering with the unaccustomed cold.

Goods were cheaper at the Italian town of Bellagio and Roger spent some of the Italian lire he had had the foresight to bring with him. After a cup of creamy coffee to warm them, they bought a few gifts from the many souvenir shops.

Tamsin, tiring of the expensive and stylish clothes she had brought with her at her uncle's insistence, bought several tops and shirts and a couple of pairs of jeans. One of these she put on after retiring to the ladies' room on the ferry boat during the return journey across Lake Como.

They arrived back at the hotel in time for dinner to find that the lounge was filled again with the visiting delegates. Tamsin had hoped to slip up to her room unnoticed. She was windblown and cold. Her new shirt and jeans—the kind of clothes she often wore at home—made her look a very different person from the girl who, until now, had worn expensive outfits bought with her uncle's money.

Sarne was in the centre of a group who were talking animatedly. From the way he was listening and then speaking, he was probably translating from one language to another. Nevertheless, he saw her enter between Roger and Douglas. Douglas's arm was across her shoulders while Roger held her hand.

Sarne's eyes scrutinised her from head to foot and, brief

though his examination was, it was plain that he had noticed the change in her style of dress. Tamsin clutched her parcels and made for the stairs, calling to her companions that she would see them at dinner.

In her room, the mirror reflected a dishevelled, bright-eyed young woman in a tight-fitting tee-shirt and even closer-fitting denim jeans. Yes, she thought with satisfaction, this is the real 'me'. I don't care what the other guests think, least of all Professor Sarne Brand, I'm not changing for dinner! If Douglas and Roger can dress like this, so can I.

They had not arrived when Tamsin went downstairs and mixed with the crowds. Panicking because she was alone and therefore unprotected from the man she had somehow come to fear as well as love, she sought for him, hoping she would not find him.

He was making his way purposefully through the crowds towards her. Like an animal eluding its enemy, she looked for cover. There was none. She was trapped.

'Where have you been today?' His voice had an edge to it. His scrutiny of her outfit and the masculine appreciation of the shape beneath the unconventional clothes made her prickle.

'I don't think it's any of your business,' she retorted.

Blue-grey eyes challenged brown. Brown eyes won and the blue-grey fell under the hardness in the brown. His eyes made a second tour of her person, and she began to burn at the derisive glint her appearance produced in his gaze.

'I repeat,' he said, 'where have you been?'

She gritted her teeth. 'Out.' She looked at him with defiance and saw that the lips which had kissed her countless times had tightened. She decided that the truth was, in the circumstances, less inciting than prevarication. 'With Douglas and Roger.'

'Those two adolescent types who picked you up?'

She blazed, 'They're not adolescent types and you should know it! Your work brings you into contact with young men like them all the time, doesn't it? They're the salt of the earth and——'

'And where you're concerned,' Sarne cut in curtly, 'they're on to a good thing and *you* know it. You hardly know them, yet you dine with them, drink with them, spend the day with them——'

'I hardly "knew" you, did I?' she hit back. 'Yet I went around with you. You—you k-kissed me——'

With a cynical smile, 'You allowed me to.'

She swung away. 'You're impossible!'

'Hey, Juliet!' Roger called from the stairs. 'Sorry we're late.'

'Hi, Roger, Douglas...' Tamsin forced a note of pleasure into her voice and heard hard footsteps stride away.

During dinner, Tamsin's companions kept up a constant stream of banter which had her laughing her way through the meal. Sarne dined with the others, but Nona Hampton was beside him.

After coffee, Douglas said, 'Come up to our room, Tamsin, and talk about what we're going to do this evening.'

Tamsin could see no possible reason why she should not do so and went up in the lift with them. They walked arm in arm, three abreast across the third-floor corridor, staying that way while Roger found the key in his pocket.

As he pushed the key into the lock, someone passed them, making for one of the other bedrooms. Fearfully, and knowing as if by instinct who it was, Tamsin looked over her shoulder. Sarne Brand, just along the corridor, was feeling in his pocket for his key and, at the same time, turning an incisive and scathing look in her direction. 'Cheap,' it said, 'cheap and easy to get.'

Roger led the way into the room and they moved together, still linked. At last they uncoupled and Douglas made for the mini-bar, asking Roger for the key.

'Drinks all round,' he said. 'The prof's mad with jealousy. Let's offer a toast to your future with the learned languages expert.'

Tamsin would have cried if she had not laughed. Her future with Sarne Brand! When she was no more to him than a casual 'pick-up'. Hadn't he implied that, where these two young men were concerned, that was all she was?

At first, Tamsin refused the drink they offered her, but when they said, 'We've got news for you, Juliet—your two Romeos will be moving on tomorrow evening, so let's drink to our short friendship,' she had no choice but to accept the glass they gave her.

Her heart dived. After tomorrow, she would be alone again. Soon the conference would be over, too. Would Sarne end his vacation and return home—wherever his home might be?

'We'll go and visit that villa they're advertising at reception,' said Roger. 'Then we'll pack our things and catch the post bus to the next youth hostel along the route. Come with us, Tamsin, to the Villa Magnifico—oh!' He assumed a mock-Italian accent and moved his fingers in a gesture of appreciation.

'I'd love to,' Tamsin said, and if there was a note of defiance in her voice, they did not notice.

'Good,' said Douglas. 'Now, what shall we do this evening?'

'Let's patronise the night spots,' said Roger. 'Let's all be devils and——'

'I don't think I'll come,' Tamsin began, but Roger broke in,

'Come on, Juliet. You're a big girl now. We'll play big brothers and hold your hand.'

'Play Juliet's brother?' said Douglas. 'When I'm supposed to be her Romeo? What do you take me for? And if you tell me, I'll——' He took up a menacing position, fists raised. Roger responded immediately in a similar way and Tamsin laughed delightedly at the byplay.

She stood up, pretending to act as intermediary and trying to part them, putting a hand on their chests—and a tall, dark-haired man passed the door, which they had all forgotten to close.

His head was turned in their direction and as he went by, he took in the situation at a glance. Or rather, Tamsin thought, removing her hands from the young men, and burning with embarrassment, what Sarne, with his cynical attitude to life, no doubt assumed to be the situation.

'Come on, Tamsin,' they coaxed. 'Give us the pleasure of your company on our last night here.'

'I'll have to change,' she said, giving in.

'Of course,' they both said at once and eyeing her simultaneously with very male admiration. For the first time since she had met them, she felt self-conscious and made for the door.

In her wardrobe was a dress which, although not ankle-length, would be suitable for the occasion. The material was patterned with autumn-tinted leaves against a white background. The neckline was high and the sleeves ended with a frill at her wrists. The effectiveness was in the expert cut and the seductive way it followed every line and curve of her figure.

She put on make-up but gave up trying to bring any order to her hair. She slipped her feet into white sandals and draped a jacket over her arm.

When Tamsin tapped on Roger's and Douglas's door and received the invitation to enter, two pairs of admiring eyes and two synchronised wolf whistles greeted her. To her surprise, the young men had contrived to look not only neat and tidy, but presentable, too. From the depths of their rucksacks they must each have tugged a pair of cord slacks in good condition.

With a map of the town in their hands and with Tamsin

between them, they swung out of the hotel entrance drive and made for the promenade. A short walk brought them to a side street in which, the advertisement on the back of the map indicated, the night club called La Cantina—The Cellar—was to be found.

Tamsin was glad to find herself alone in the ladies' room. The mirrors around the walls showed a slim, timid young figure, looking around and wondering what she was doing there. What mad moment had made her decide to accompany Roger and Douglas to such a sophisticated place? It was not her scene at all.

As she pushed at the door, she had to quell a sudden desire to seize her coat from the attendant and return to the hotel. Only a wish not to let her companions down made her stay. They were waiting for her patiently. Beside the men and women who were milling about in the entrance lobby, they looked young, slightly dazzled and touchingly vulnerable.

They were not the sophisticated men they had pretended to be and Tamsin guessed that a visit to such a place was a first time for them as well as herself. But being young, they'd been determined to savour, within reason, as many levels of experience as came their way.

Tamsin realised she could count herself lucky to be accompanied to such a place by two young men who undoubtedly possessed integrity and trustworthiness. This much she had learnt about them in the course of their short acquaintance with her.

Douglas put his arm about her waist and Tamsin sensed that it was a purely protective gesture. Roger led the way into a darkened room whose lighting came from Chinese lanterns suspended from the ceiling. This was augmented by coloured lamps on tables around the dancing area, but the whole atmosphere was one of mystery and a subdued excitement.

Couples were dancing to the slow, sensual rhythm of the

music. Some were so close they clung together. The air was heavy with exhaled smoke, perfume and the smell of alcohol. Tamsin had never felt so out of place in her life.

'Dance?' asked Douglas, holding out his arms.

Tamsin nodded, glad to be doing something, anything to rid herself of the strange feeling of guilt which had settled on her since she had entered the place. What was she doing there with two comparatively strange young men —here in a night club in a foreign country and in an atmosphere which was entirely alien to her and which somehow offended—she had to admit it—her slightly puritan attitude to life.

'Not too close,' she whispered to Douglas, as his arms went round her.

He laughed. 'I bet Juliet didn't say that to Romeo!' Tamsin smiled at him and he pulled her closer. Something in her face seemed to have prompted the action.

'Why did you do that?' she asked, a little affronted.

'Do you really not realise how attractive you are?' She shrugged. 'Doesn't it matter to you?'

Yes, she thought, but only where a certain man is concerned. One man only. But she couldn't tell Douglas that.

'It hasn't helped me get a job,' she said.

'Next time,' Douglas said, laughing, 'pin a picture of yourself to the application form. That should get you an interview *and* the job!'

'My turn,' said Roger, cutting in smoothly. 'You can't keep Juliet to yourself. There are two Romeos here this evening, not just one.' Douglas lifted his shoulders and surrendered his partner.

'Enjoying the experience?' Roger asked, looking at her with an expression which was very similar, Tamsin noticed with amusement, to Douglas's—admiration combined with a heightened consciousness of their own masculinity.

They had brought her there. To say 'No, I'm not,' would

upset them, so she nodded—and tripped over Roger's feet. He laughed and pulled her close. She had told Douglas, 'Not too close' and he had complied with her request. She had not thought to ask the same of Roger. But Roger was different. There was no doubt that his possession of a wealthier background had given him something—poise, self-assurance—that Douglas had missed out on.

'Would Juliet condescend to kiss Romeo Mark Two?' Tamsin looked up at Roger with surprise. With his lips he caught hers, which were parted to protest. 'Thanks,' he said, grinning. 'I'll wrap that up and take it home as a souvenir. You don't blame me for trying my luck, do you?'

Tamsin had to laugh. She shook her head.

The music stopped and Douglas reappeared. 'Me now.' He shouldered Roger out of the way. The music started again. 'If he can do that, so can I.'

'Do what?'

'This.' His lips swooped and caught a kiss from the upturned mouth.

'Look, I——'

'Sorry, I'll behave. But if there are kisses being given away, I wanted to be in on the act, too.'

Tamsin smiled up at him. 'I know we haven't all known each other very long, but you've both been very kind to me. I'd have been very lonely if you two——'

'Say no more.' He bent down and whispered, 'I don't know if you're aware of it, but we're under supervision. The prof's here. But sad to say, he's accompanied.' Tamsin's heart skidded to a stop and then beat on heavily.

'You mean Sarne Brand's here?' Douglas nodded. 'When—when did he come in?'

'Just after we did. Roger pointed him out to me. We thought you'd seen him.'

So Sarne had been a witness, if he had been looking their way—which, according to Douglas, he had been—to the laughs, the kisses, the changes of partner.

'Did you say,' she whisperd, 'he's got someone with him?' Douglas nodded. 'A—a woman?'

'Who else? And what a woman!'

'Is she—is she tall, dark-haired, very slim? There's a woman interpreter staying at the hotel he's friendly with.'

Douglas shook his head. 'She's medium height—a bit shorter than you—dark-haired, yes, but slim? We-ell, I'd hardly call her that. Boy, has she got plenty—if you know what I mean! If you want a quick look at her, I'll swing you round. There, over in the corner. Quick, while the prof's attention is on the bar.'

Tamsin looked and saw at Sarne's side a woman she had never seen before. She was a black-haired, beautiful young woman and she was looking, not at the bar, but at the small band of musicians who played the music for dancing. Was she longing to be on the dance floor and in Sarne's arms?

She did, as Douglas had said, possess everything a man could wish for in a woman. Her dress was long and a deep yellow. Her hair was coiled in a sophisticated knot at the back of her head. Her eyes, like Sarne's, were long-lashed and, no doubt when the occasion demanded, heart-melting in a feminine way. It was plain that she shared Sarne's Italian inheritance.

Without hearing the music, and forgetting with whom she was dancing, Tamsin's feet moved automatically. Another woman on Sarne Brand's list! How could she, Tamsin, ever have considered herself worthy of Sarne's exclusive—and special—attention? It was plain that his preference was for dark-haired women. How could a blonde like herself ever stand a chance with him?

'Like to sit down?' Douglas asked. 'It's obvious you're not with me. I shouldn't have told you, should I?' he teased. 'You seem to have crept back into your shell.'

Tamsin smiled ruefully. 'Sorry. I didn't realise ...' She sighed as she sank into her seat at the table. Roger was missing.

Douglas, guessing where he had gone, excused himself. 'We'll be right back. You won't be alone for more than half a minute.'

That half-minute's solitude was enough for Tamsin to be noticed by a greying man sitting alone. She saw his eyes on her as he drank and became uncomfortably aware of the true nature of the place she had come to with her two companions. When Roger and Douglas had been beside her, she had not noticed the slight air of decadence, the tired sophistication of the patrons, the over-familiarity of the looks which were coming her way from the male customers.

When the grey-haired man stood and made his way towards her, stopping at her table, she gazed up at him petrified. He spoke in a language she guessed to be Italian. She shook her head, signifying that she did not understand. His hands moved, motioning her towards the dance floor.

Tamsin looked round for Roger and Douglas. There was no sign of them. Over the other side Sarne had his companion in his arms and was dancing with his back to the room.

The man caught at Tamsin's wrist and pulled her up. Not wishing to make a scene, she complied. When he began to urge her into the midst of the dancers, she shook her head furiously, hoping he would understand. It seemed he had no wish to understand and tugged harder.

'No, no, thank you,' she said. She racked her brains. What was the Italian for no? She began to resist. 'No, thank you, I don't *want* to dance...'

'Tamsin!' A hand gripped her shoulder and tugged her away. So Sarne had come to her aid. If only it had been Roger or Douglas! Sarne spoke sharply in fast Italian to the man, who shrugged resignedly, bowed deeply to Tamsin and wandered back to his table.

Sarne turned, manhandled Tamsin into his arms and pushed her unceremoniously on to the dance floor. 'What the hell are you doing here?' he said between his teeth. 'You know what kind of a place this is?'

If only he would stop being so rough! 'If it's that bad,' she said sulkily, feeling an immediate response within her as her body made contact with his, 'why are you here? And why did you bring your lady friend here?'

'It's none of your business. But I'd like to know what possessed those two young fools to escort you to such a place. Or,' he gritted, 'do I take a guess? I saw the kisses, I saw the familiarity...'

'You're reading far too much into the situation,' she protested fiercely. 'They're thoroughly nice, good-natured, high-principled——'

'What's this,' he sneered, 'a character reference for a job? There's no need for you to sell them to me. But you've done a pretty good job of selling yourself.'

Tamsin twisted away, using all her energies. 'You're despicable to suggest—Anyway,' she saw the two young men seated at their table, 'they're back. They'll hear you——'

A hand gripped her wrist. 'Come with me. We can continue our discussion outside.'

As she lagged behind Sarne on his journey to the door, Tamsin cast a despairing glance over her shoulder. Roger gave her the thumbs-up sign and Douglas clasped his hands over his head in a gesture of triumph. They didn't understand, she thought bleakly. It wasn't what they assumed—that Sarne was so bewitched by her that he had to have her to himself.

'Now,' Sarne pushed her into a dark corner—there were many dark corners, she discovered, and most of them were occupied by entwined couples—'enlighten me,' he said sarcastically. 'Explain to me your exact relationship to those two men.'

'Friends, just friends, that's all we are. Don't you remember? They were trying to get a lift outside the hotel. I passed them on my way out—you saw them, too—and they were still there when I came back. They got fed up and decided to stay here. That's all there is to it. They—they saw I was lonely, so——'

'Ah, so that's it—the line you put across so successfully on me. Quite omitting, of course, to tell me that there was someone waiting patiently, trustingly, back home.'

'They're kind,' she said desperately, 'they're——'

'As "kind" as I was to you? And will you repay them as you did me, only more so—going all the way? After all, there are two of them, and it will require more effort on your part to satisfy——'

She drew a breath from her depths, lifted a hand and brought it stingingly against his cheek. His eyes blazed and the same hand that had hit his cheek now pressed in dismay against her own. What had she done?

He caught her wrists in a savage grip, jerking them down to her sides. 'By heaven, you little fiend, you'll be sorry you did that. You'll pay, my girl, and that's a promise!'

He swung back to the noise and the crowds, leaving her in the shadowed corner. Her lips trembled, her eyes filled as she massaged her bruised wrists. She had hurt him, and not only physically. She had wounded his pride, and she trembled at the thought of what he might do to get equal with her.

CHAPTER SEVEN

TAMSIN slept fitfully, waking in the morning with a feeling of dread. The remembrance of what she had done to Sarne the evening before had not left her thoughts, and had even invaded her dreams.

The rest of the time they had spent at the night club had

been a blur, with Roger and Douglas doing their best to restore her good humour.

When she had told them what she had done, they had cheered, quietly but ironically, quoting the old saying about the path of true love never running smooth. Her efforts to persuade them that love didn't enter into her relationship with Sarne Brand were in vain. They had refused to believe her.

As they had left their table to return to the hotel, Sarne had watched them go. Tamsin had stolen a glance at his face, but it had been without expression. Her companions had walked her back to the hotel and seen her to her door, making arrangements to meet her at breakfast.

Tamsin dressed in the jeans she had bought and a sleeveless striped top. The expensive clothes she had brought with her hung unused in the wardrobe. She felt much happier dressed as she did at home and in the fashion that people like Douglas and Roger adopted.

They had not yet appeared when she helped herself to breakfast on the terrace and chose a table at which to sit. Almost immediately, Sarne entered, dressed impeccably in a suit, making her feel out of place and inelegant in her youthful outfit. He collected his breakfast and passed her table, wishing her a cool good morning.

Mr and Mrs van Ruyter came on to the terrace and with their plates in their hands, stopped by Tamsin's table. 'Are you off somewhere nice today?' Mr van Ruyter asked.

'We're going to have a look at the Villa Magnifico,' Tamsin told them.

'It's well worth a visit,' Mrs van Ruyter said. 'Are you going alone, or are your two young friends accompanying you?' She looked around. 'Are they still staying here?'

'Yes, but they move on this evening. We're all going to the villa, though.'

They hoped Tamsin and her friends enjoyed themselves and they went on their way. Since Sarne was sitting within hearing distance, Tamsin knew he must have heard the conversation.

The Villa Magnifico was situated on the hills above Morcote. It stood in a clearing in the midst of a circle of trees and surrounded by gardens with exotic flowers and plants. The coach stopped in the forecourt of the great white building and access to the villa was through a series of stone archways.

Stone steps to the right and left, bounded by intricate ironwork, led upwards each side to pause at an alcove in which statues from mythology stood. Three flights led to the entrance doors, one on each side, and the building joined at last in a magnificent façade of painted walls and carved figures.

The group of sightseers was met by a smiling woman of medium height. Her carefully groomed appearance, her air of self-assurance and gently superior bearing, placed her in a category above that of hired guides. In her smile of welcome was also the look of pride of possession. Was she, Tamsin wondered, the owner of this building, its magnificence echoed in its name?

The woman, who introduced herself as Signora Bezzurri, spoke first in German, switching to French and then to English. She was, she told the assembled company, a resident but not the owner of the Villa. She lived there with her adopted daughter, Nicoletta, and—she spoke with disarming frankness—they paid no rent. In return, they acted as guides to the many people who wished to see the beauties of the Villa Magnifico.

While it was not large when compared with the great palazzos, the treasures it contained, she informed the visitors with pride, were worth a great deal of money and were, in some cases, so valuable they were beyond price.

Here, she told them, leading the way into a high-ceilinged room with a glittering crystal chandelier, was the parlour, and it contained many treasures. Against a wall stood a harp with intricate carvings. Her ancestors, she said, were musical and used this as a music room.

She led them through a doorway into the dining-room where a long shining wooden table was arranged with place settings for twenty people, while at intervals down the centre stood silver candelabra. On the wall hung an ancient tapestry and around it there were portraits painted by world-famous artists.

Through the library—the contents of which, she explained, was worth much money—into the main drawing-room and Signora Bezzurri indicated the great marble fireplace with its carvings and above it silver ornaments on a shelf. All round the walls hung paintings and again, she explained, they were the works of famous Italian and other renowned artists.

The visitors followed the woman up a stone staircase, the walls of which were covered with frescoes of figures caught in movement, still, yet almost alive through the brilliance of the painter. In the main bedroom was a canopied four-poster bed, each post being carved and twisting to the top. The bedhead was similarly decorated and the quilted covers and draperies told of dedicated hands lovingly sewing them in centuries past.

Tamsin lingered at the window and saw a dazzling view of Lake Lugano. The Villa, it seemed, although approached by means of a drive and gardens on one side, was in reality poised on the top of a cliff which dropped away sharply to the water's edge. Its starkness was softened by small conifers, bushes and brilliantly coloured plants.

As she turned from the view, Tamsin saw standing in the doorway through which they had come the figure of a young woman—a black-haired, brown-eyed, beautiful young woman who, only a few hours before, had been dancing in Sarne Brand's arms.

It was plain that she was no visitor. She had the same air of belonging about her as Signora Bezzurri. So this was the daughter of whom the woman had spoken. This girl lived here and this girl knew Sarne Brand.

Douglas, returning through another door to look for Tamsin, followed her gaze and came up against the young woman at whom Tamsin was staring. His eyes, too, opened wide. That the young woman recognised Tamsin was obvious. What Tamsin could not understand was the lack of any feeling—resentment or jealousy—in the girl's eyes.

After all, hadn't Sarne left his companion last night to dance with another woman—herself—even taking her outside? Perhaps he had explained his action to his companion, even going so far as to tell her—truthfully—that he and the girl he had danced with had had a violent quarrel.

The young woman turned away and disappeared. Tamsin, stunned, followed Douglas down the stairs. He whispered, 'There she is, your rival!' and grinned.

The visitors had gathered again in the main drawing-room. Standing at Signora Bezzurri's side was the young woman and Signora Bezzurri was introducing her to the crowd. She pointed to a large painting in a gilt frame on the wall above the magnificent fireplace. How, Tamsin wondered, had she missed it, that of all the things in the room!

'The owner of the Villa Magnifico,' the Signora said. It was a portrait of Sarne Brand.

He was dressed in a dark suit. His pose—arms across his body, elbows cupped by each hand, legs slightly apart—was one of arrogance, pride and challenge. Yes, there, too, was the autocratic air, the aristocratic bearing which Tamsin had perceived the moment she had set eyes upon him. His half-smile tantalised, lifting a veil on the charm which, as Tamsin now knew to her cost, when exercised, was irresistible. It hinted, too, at a hardness and obduracy which, when encountered, as Tamsin also knew by experience, instilled fear, despair and a sense of helplessness against its inflexibility.

144

'He is my nephew and the fiancé of my beautiful adopted daughter, Nicoletta, here by my side. Before very long they are to be married.'

It was time to go downstairs to dinner, but Tamsin lingered in her room. She had changed into a dress which was pale blue, short-sleeved and simply styled. As usual, her hair hung in a cluster of long curls about her throat.

She was not looking at her reflection, however. Instead, she gazed out of the window at the mountains as the sun picked out and gilded patches of forest, throwing into shadow rocky slopes and red-roofed houses which clung to the hillsides.

Her mind was elsewhere—in the Villa Magnifico, with all its riches, its history of past glories—and its present owner. All the pieces fitted into place. The fleeting impression she had had on her first meeting with Sarne Brand had not been wrong. Along with the aristocratic air had been the slightly impatient manner of a man used to clicking his fingers and having his wishes obeyed.

It must have been instilled in his personality by centuries of breeding, by the richness of his environment and by the security and self-assurance to which such richness gives rise in those fortunate enough to be born into it.

So Sarne was a rich man and as such, could afford to play around with other women—after all, he was not yet married, was he? He could afford to live in the luxurious Hotel Tranquillité for an indefinite period. He could afford to make love to a girl like Tamsin Selby—and any other woman who took his fancy—knowing that, sooner or later, she would go out of his life. All the time he knew that, waiting patiently and submissively in the background, was the girl—the beautiful, dark-haired girl—he intended to marry.

The dining-room seemed curiously empty, like, Tamsin

thought miserably, my heart. The Dutch couple passed her table on their way to their own.

'It's an extra long session of the conference today,' they told her. 'It ends officially tonight. Tomorrow the delegates will go sightseeing if they wish and gather for a final farewell in the conference hall tomorrow evening. Mr Brand told us.'

'He also said,' Mr van Ruyter added, 'how glad he would be when it was all over. He has worked extremely hard, it seems. He told us that the stresses and strains of such work on a skilled interpreter as he is are tremendous.'

'And he's been doing the work of two, remember,' Mrs van Ruyter said.

Mr Brand, it seemed, Tamsin thought bitterly, as the couple left her, had once again told them far more than he had told Tamsin Selby. But she was beneath his contempt, wasn't she, whereas he no doubt held the van Ruyters in high regard.

Tamsin consulted the menu without really seeing it. Douglas and Roger had gone, their rucksacks on their backs, and were making for the next youth hostel on their route.

They had exchanged addresses with her and had made her promise to write to them when she returned home. On the way back from the Villa Magnifico they had commiserated with her. 'But,' they had said, 'fight for him, Tamsin. He's not married yet, is he?'

Tamsin had smiled and shaken her head. After what had happened between them the night before, she doubted if Sarne would speak to her again. Maybe that was what he had meant by saying that she would be sorry for what she had done to him and that his way of 'making her pay' would be to ignore her.

The evening was fine. Tamsin, feeling unaccountably restless, changed into jeans and shirt top and went for a walk. By the time she returned, the delegates were drifting in. She looked round, but there was no sign of Sarne. In her room, Tamsin removed her jacket, then wondered what to do. It was time, she decided, to write a few cards to friends and relations. There was a display of colour postcards at reception and she left her door on the catch and went down to the entrance hall.

As she approached the display of cards, Sarne Brand came out of the dining-room. He was alone and, glancing quickly at him, Tamsin thought that he looked tired.

'Miss Selby?' The girl behind the desk was at the switchboard. 'A phone call for you. Mr Williams from London. Would you please take the call in the office here, as you did before?'

Yes, Tamsin thought, glancing over her shoulder, her heart throbbing, Sarne had heard. His eyes were narrow, his lips twisted and cynical. The boy-friend again, he was probably thinking. Tamsin hurried into the small office and spoke her name.

'Tamsin, love,' she heard, 'how are you? It's your uncle here, as if you didn't know! Look, love, I'm coming over in a day or two, just to see how things are going and say "hallo" to my lovely niece. How're you feeling, lass? All right now?'

Tamsin assured him she had fully recovered.

'Everything all right at your end? You know what I mean! Not just the hotel but—didn't you say something about a young man?'

Tamsin laughed dismissingly, and congratulated herself on her acting. 'Oh, that! It's——'

'All right, lass, you don't have to tell your uncle everything. Your mum and dad send their love. A certain Mr Bill Williams will be seeing you soon.' He rang off, laughing.

Tamsin lingered at reception, but there was no sign of Sarne. She bought a few postcards and made her way slowly upstairs. So, she thought, in a few days, her uncle would be joining her. The knowledge was something of a relief.

Not only would it mean an end to her loneliness, but he would act as a very solid barrier between herself and Sarne Brand. What harm could Sarne do her with her uncle in the way? How could he 'make her pay' for what she had done when Uncle William was there to shield her?

Tamsin pushed open her door—and gasped. A door to the balcony was open and Sarne Brand leant on the parapet.

'How——?' she asked, and then remembered. She had left her door on the catch. 'What are you doing here?' Her heart began to pound.

Sarne looked lazily over his shoulder. 'Enjoying the scenery.'

'You can do that in your own room.' She dropped the postcards on to a table.

'Ah, but there the scenery's only good outside. Here, it's good inside, too.' He grinned provocatively and turned back to the view. 'Come and join me. Tell me, how did you enjoy your visit to the Villa Magnifico? Did it, in your opinion, live up to its name?'

She stood at the balcony door and said challengingly, 'You didn't tell me you owned it.'

He continued to gaze at the mountains which darkened as the sun went down. 'If I had, would it have made any difference to our relationship last week? Would it, perhaps, have made you more—willing?'

A pause, then in answer, 'Don't you know me well enough by now to realise that I'm not—well, like that?'

Harshly he said, 'Aren't you? How smooth you are when you tell lies.'

She flinched but was silent. What was the use of denying the implied accusation? The last time he had been in her room, he had demonstrated by word and deed exactly what he thought of her morals. She was as powerless now as she had been then to correct him. But at least she could challenge.

'The villa is beautiful. And so is your fiancée.'

He swung round and his eyes narrowed. 'Who told you that?'

'Signora Bezzurri, your aunt. It seems she's so proud of your forthcoming marriage to her adopted daughter, she's announcing it to everyone who goes there.' Tamsin added sarcastically, 'It will save you the bother, and the cost, won't it, of inserting an announcement in the appropriate newspapers? Not that you have to worry about money. After all, the villa's yours, too, isn't it, like the girl who goes with it?'

'So my aunt's telling the world, is she?'

'Don't worry, Professor Brand, she isn't mentioning names. She merely refers to you as "her nephew".'

He gritted his teeth and started towards her. She retreated and he checked himself, contenting himself with saying, 'Why the sudden formality?'

Tamsin picked up the postcards, inspecting them one by one. 'I should treat you with more respect now, shouldn't I? Not only are you a university professor, which I didn't know when we first got acquainted, but you're the illustrious owner of a richly endowed, magnificent equivalent of an English stately home.'

'Sarcasm ill becomes you, Miss Selby.'

She flashed at him, smiling provokingly, 'Now who's being formal?' She hoped her inner turmoil did not show. It would be extremely imprudent to allow him to guess how frightened she was of him.

He seemed to have second thoughts and turned back to the view. What had he been going to do? she wondered. Repay her in kind for her treatment of him at the night club?

When would he go? 'I have some postcards to write,' she said, as coolly as she could manage. Would he take the hint?

'Go ahead,' was the careless reply. 'Forget I'm here.'

Her heart sank. How could she get him out of her room?

His presence was disturbing her profoundly, her anxiety as to his intention increasing every minute. Was this his way of making her 'sorry'? By inflicting himself on her uninvited?

As if to underline her suspicion, he strolled into the room and to her side. He held out his hand. 'The key to your mini-bar?' The autocratic manner was there again, demanding instant obedience. If giving him the key would humour him, then he would have the key.

As it passed between them, their eyes met and held. He must have seen in hers the rebellion at his arrogance, the annoyance she was forced to quell in order to give in to his demand. His mocking smile grew and she knew he was fully aware of his command of the situation.

He turned to the drinks cabinet and she caught the shadows round his eyes, the slight droop of his broad shoulders. Loving him as she did, she was sensitive to his every mood and she knew then how tired he must be feeling. Her heart went out to him—until she remembered that he had spent the previous evening with his fiancée.

If the hour at which he had gone to bed, on top of a day's demanding work, had been a late one, it was his business entirely. And if today had tired him excessively on top of all that, then what could she do about it?

'Join me in a drink?' he asked. Tamsin shook her head and he lifted careless shoulders. He selected a miniature bottle and relocked the cabinet. She heard the chink of money and the clatter as he dropped it on to the cabinet top. She knew better than to argue with him about money in his present mood.

He removed the top from the bottle and without bothering to find a glass, put the bottle to his lips. He drank the liquid down, wiped his mouth with the back of his hand and threw the bottle away. There was a lazy, devil-may-care attitude about him that had Tamsin biting her lip. What was he playing at? He was acting in a way that had her pulses hammering.

He moved and she watched, unbelievingly. He removed his tie and his shoes, unfastened most of the buttons of his shirt and stretched out full-length on the second bed. He lifted his hands and rested his head on them against the pillow. Then he turned to her and smiled. It was smug, it was derisive and it was full of self-satisfaction. Most of all, it was a smile of victory.

'Quits,' he murmured.

'What'—she moistened her lips—'what are you doing?'

'What does it look like? Making myself comfortable for the night.'

Her face flamed. 'For the *night*?' Her voice rose to a shriek. 'You can't stay here. You *can't*!'

'Can't I? How do you intend to stop me? Carry me to my room?'

'I'll—I'll phone the management.'

He indicated the telephone. 'Call them. I dare you to.' He watched as she lifted the receiver. 'What are you going to say?' he mocked. His voice mimicked hers. 'There's a man in my room. It's Professor Brand and he won't go. What can I do?'

Tamsin thrust back the receiver. 'Will you *please* go?' In spite of herself, her voice sounded tearful. 'If it gets around that you stayed here——'

'Your reputation—your so precious reputation,' she flinched at the sarcasm, 'will be in shreds, won't it? All right, *I'll* phone the management.' He turned on to his side and seized the telephone which stood on a shelf above the beds. Before she could stop him, he had dialled reception.

'No!' she shrieked, trying to wrench the receiver from him. His hand gripped her wrist and held it.

'Reception?' he said. 'I'm speaking from Miss Selby's room. I want breakfast for two brought up here in the morning at eight-thirty, please. Yes, room one hundred. Thanks.' He replaced the receiver, released her wrist and settled back against the pillows. 'Quits again,' he murmured with a grin. 'I told you I'd make you sorry for what you did last night.' He rubbed the cheek she had hit.

'Look,' she said, unable to prevent the tears springing to her eyes and trying to swallow the lump in her throat, 'I'm sorry, I'm *sorry*. I—I promise I'll never do it again.' As soon as she said it she knew how stupid it sounded.

He closed his eyes. 'You'll never get the chance, my girl.'

The apology had plainly made no difference. It seemed he intended to remain exactly where he was. Tamsin accepted at last that there was nothing she could do. She could not bundle him out—his strength was greater than hers. She couldn't, it seemed, even appeal to his better nature.

The thought of his staying the night there made her tremble inwardly. Would he try by words or deeds to persuade her——? Looking at him, she knew that in his present devilish, slightly reckless mood, nothing was impossible. And hadn't she, last week, allowed him to make ardent love to her without even trying to repel him?

She decided to change her tactics. If she let him know how much his presence worried her, he would gloat even more about his successful revenge. In any case, she could not bring herself to plead with him. If she pretended that she was not at all perturbed by his being there, if she prepared herself for bed as if she were alone, that would surely not only call his bluff, but it would take away the pleasure he was feeling for having so successfully 'made her pay' for her audacity in slapping his face.

So with an elaborate shrug she pulled the curtains and looked at the time. She glanced at him through her lashes and found that he was smiling, so she returned his smile. Did his eyes narrow fractionally or was it her imagination?

With a brave attempt to appear unconcerned, she switched on the radio. Soft music played, filling the tense silence. She picked up a book and sat on the side of her own bed, flicking the pages. Some time she would have to start undressing. The idea filled her with alarm. Anything to delay that moment ...

'Would you—would you like anything else to drink?' she asked. Why did her voice sound so timid?

'No, thanks. But don't let me stop you.'

So that was no use. She threw the book down, switched off the radio and turned on him. 'I want to go to bed, Sarne.'

He grinned. 'Don't let me stop you.'

She gritted her teeth. 'All right, I won't.' She turned her back on him, began to unbutton her shirt, stopped as she became aware of what she was doing and turned back to him. 'Please, Sarne,' she whispered, 'will you go now?'

'No.'

She swung away from him again, closed her eyes momentarily, then one by one the buttons came undone. When the shirt was half-way off, she stopped again, seeking courage. He had seen her, as many other people had, in a bikini. Now, under the shirt was a bra, and instead of the brief bikini pants she wore jeans. Therefore, she argued, she was wearing more at that moment than when she had been in the swimming pool.

The shirt slipped off and she flung it on a chair.

'Tamsin?' She was still. 'Turn round.' So he was intent on humiliating her still further. If she refused, that would be another point to him. Slowly, hugging herself with her arms—somehow she must hide from him her trembling limbs—she turned towards him.

But there was no tenderness in his regard, as she had thought there might be, no admiration of her femininity. There was, instead, a hardness in his eyes, a taut cynicism about his lips which shocked her.

'So my being here doesn't inhibit you. Which can only mean one thing—you're used to undressing with a man in your bedroom. Your lover, I suppose, who's taken the trouble—and be damned to the expense—of phoning you *twice* all the way from London.'

'I tell you,' she said tremulously, 'I haven't got a "lover".'

His whole body stiffened. 'Then who the hell was it who did call you tonight and the other time? Santa Claus?'

'It was my——' No, she could not tell him. If she said 'my uncle', he would ask questions—why, for what reason—and why not your parents? They would be questions she couldn't answer because of her promise to her uncle to tell no one who she was.

'Don't tell me it was a relative,' he went on, 'because I wouldn't believe you. If your parents are such ordinary folk as you tell me they are, they wouldn't be able to afford it.' He rolled on to his side and supported himself on his elbow. 'And don't tell me you had the charges reversed, to be put on your account, because again I wouldn't believe you.' He eyed her unsparingly, the curving, shivering shapeliness of her, her flushed face and tousled hair. 'You're an out-of-work teacher, aren't you?'

Tamsin's heart, already racing, stumbled and pounded on. 'How do you know?'

'In the bar the other evening. I heard you tell those student-types who stayed here. I was sitting near you, as you may remember.'

'All right,' she unwrapped her arms from her body and immediately regretted the action. His eyes wandered over her slender form, dwelling lazily on the pronounced rise and fall of her breasts. She seized the discarded shirt and draped it defensively across her shoulders. 'You know I'm unemployed. So where does that get us?'

'It means, *signorina*,' his dark eyes flashed, 'that as such you couldn't possibly afford to stay here unless you're being subsidised by someone, almost certainly a man, with money to spare, and for one reason only—in payment for,' his eyes half-closed reflectively, 'I was going to say "services", but I'll be charitable and call it "the pleasures" you give him.'

'You've got an imagination like a sewer!' she flung at him. She seized her nightdress and ran towards the bathroom.

He was off the bed and after her, tearing off the shirt and throwing it aside. His hands spanned her waist until the tips of his fingers made contact. Her flesh was compressed so tightly she bit her lip, but she would not cry out. He jerked her against him and looked her over possessively.

'So you think my mind's a sewer, do you? Then you must know what I'm thinking now. Doesn't the knowledge make you blush? But you must have passed the blushing stage long ago. So how am I to think of you? After the way you behaved with those two students—and complete strangers at that. I don't need to use my imagination. You told me everything I needed to know about you.' He released her and wandered back to the bed, flinging himself on it. 'Not to mention your behaviour with me, both in the past and now, with me in your room.'

Her hands went to her ears. 'Will you stop it!' she cried. 'Will you stop tormenting me!' The tears came. She could not control them. 'You've had your revenge. Can't you leave me alone? If you want lovemaking, if you want your sexual desires to be satisfied, why don't you go to your fiancée at the Villa Magnifico?'

'You want me to leave you alone? No, my beauty, that I simply will not do. And go to my fiancée?' He smiled and closed his eyes. 'That I certainly will do—all in good time. But in her absence,' with a mocking smile, 'I can have "another woman" to console me, can't I? It's happening all the time, my sweet.' He stretched luxuriously. 'You admitted it yourself at the start of our acquaintance. That "man-code", wasn't it, which permitted a man, whether married or not, to take exactly what he wants from any woman.' An eyebrow lifted. 'Your words exactly, weren't they?'

Tamsin slammed the bathroom door and locked it. What should she do—stay in there all night? She looked at the hard, blue-tiled floor. That was impossible. It was a long time before she found the courage to emerge, having showered and changed into her nightdress. She eased the door open, hoping desperately that Sarne had relented and gone.

He was there, stretched out on the bed. He was deeply asleep. At once her dread of what he might intend to do to her was swamped by a very different feeling, one of compassion, of understanding and, most of all, a profound and disturbing love for the man lying there, exhausted, relaxed and, in his unconsciousness, strangely vulnerable.

He was, of course, fully dressed, although his unbuttoned shirt revealed his bare chest with a mat of hair as dark as that on his head. Warm though the days might be, the nights were often chill. There was, Tamsin knew, a spare blanket in a cupboard. She took it out, unfolded it and with infinite care, spread it across Sarne's sleeping form.

He did not stir. His head was to one side, presenting, in the light of the bedside lamp, a handsome, aristocratic profile which moved her to her depths. How could she sleep with such a man beside her, a man she had grown to admire and love, in spite of the comparatively short time she had known him?

Sleep she did, however, as soon as her head touched the pillow. Maybe, she thought drowsily, it was because he was there that sleep and contentment came so easily. His fiancée could surely not resent these few snatched hours which she, Tamsin, would spend with him. They were together, but apart. They had done nothing morally wrong. Where was the immorality in lying asleep side by side ... ?

Something probed, like an echo-sounding device, into

156

her deepest dream. Whatever it was made her stir, surface and open her eyes. Someone was bending over her. A face was so near she could feel the breath on her cheek. Forgetting momentarily that she was not alone, alarm had her tense and terrified. Then she recognised the outline of the face, the way the thick hair lay across the forehead, the jutting chin, the long straight nose.

'Sarne,' she half sat up, 'what do you——?'

'*Cara*,' he murmured, 'the dawn is breaking over the mountains. Let's watch together.'

Still dazed from sleep, she obeyed automatically, pushing back the bedclothes and allowing her hand to be gripped by his. He led her to the window where he had drawn back the curtains. His arm encircled her waist and through the silky material of her nightdress she felt his hand lying caressingly on her midriff.

Her senses were heightened unbearably by his nearness, by the intimacy, by the contact of their bodies. As the sun rose, so the panorama of mountain ranges, forest-clad hills, white-walled villas and the mirror-like calmness of the lake became flooded with golden light. The clouds of night were driven from the skies and slowly, magnificently another sun-lit day came to life.

'Tamsin?' The hand about her waist moved up, encountering and cupping her breast. Another hand turned her face towards him, then rested on her throat. In the dawn light his face looked shadowed and mysterious. His shirt was free of the belt about his waist and hung loose, revealing his muscular frame. His hair had been untidied by sleep. His brown eyes caught the rays of the rising sun and reflected golden lights. There was warmth and ardour in those eyes, not the coldness to which she had had to harden herself through the past days.

He swung her round and pulled her against him. Through the flimsy fabric of her nightgown she felt his ribs pressing into her. He pulled at a bow and the neckline fell open. She held her breath in ecstasy as his caressing hand pushed its way inside. His seeking lips found hers, prising them apart and arousing in her a rising tide of passion.

Fighting for rationality, she told herself that it was the circumstances that made him behave in this way, the intimacy of a night spent together, watching the dawn lighten the sky. He did not love her. Desire, yes, a craving for sexual satisfaction, but not love, love ...

Her heart almost stopped as she remembered his threat. 'I'll make you pay,' he'd said at the night club. 'I'll make you sorry for that.' So this was part of his revenge, carefully planned, coldly calculated, catching her at her most vulnerable moment—in a dazed state, at dawn, with the air of romance all around them ...

She was drowning in his ardour, his caresses and his kisses. Her arms clung to his neck and her body strained to his. Before it became impossible to call a halt, before she did something she would never cease to regret—hadn't he a fiancée he intended to marry?—she had to do something to prevent herself from losing all restraint under the impact of his lovemaking. She had to summon her powers of resistance and prise his lips from hers, his stroking hands from her yielding, yearning body ...

From a hazy distance she heard his murmur, '*Cara*, you drive me crazy. With all my being, I desire you. I want to crush you beneath me, force you to submit, make you mine.'

In the end it was he, not she, who imposed the limits. It was as if breaking the silence by speaking had brought him back to reality. He disentangled her entwining arms and held her away. She had never seen such a light in a man's eyes, such fire, such a straining after conquest and a demand for total submission.

But it seemed he not only had the power to conquer but also to control. He must have been in complete command of his own impulses, because he put her away from him and went to the door. Then he left her.

CHAPTER EIGHT

TAMSIN did not sleep again. She lay quietly, passively, until there were movements indicating that the hotel day was beginning. She dressed and went downstairs. There was something she had to do.

A girl was on duty at reception. Tamsin approached and said, 'The breakfasts ordered for room one hundred, I—I wish to cancel them. I don't want——'

The girl laughed. 'They were cancelled last night, Miss Selby, shortly after they were ordered. Mr Brand called back and said he had only done it to tease you.'

Tamsin tried to hide her confusion. 'Oh—thanks.' She managed a smile and the girl smiled back understandingly.

So, Tamsin thought, going to the door, Sarne had relented. He must have called reception while she showered. He had cleared her reputation in other people's eyes, if not his own.

She walked by the lake until she reached the municipal park, then sat amongst the trees, watching the ferry boats plying to and fro and the motor boats stirring up spray in the early morning air.

By the time she returned to the hotel, she hoped that Sarne would have breakfasted and gone—wherever he was going. If the conference was over, maybe there would be delegates to see before they left for home. She had no appetite for food and decided against having breakfast. On her way upstairs, she met Mr and Mrs van Ruyter. They were off that afternoon, they told her.

Mrs van Ruyter said, 'Did you know, Miss Selby, that Professor Brand owns the Villa Magnifico? We went over the place yesterday and the lady guide told us. At least she referred to the owner as "her nephew" and we recognised him by that painting of him.'

Tamsin nodded, saying that she also had heard about the owner in the same way.

'And,' Mrs van Ruyter went on commiseratingly, 'Mr Brand is an engaged man. What a pity for you! We were match-making, my husband and I, and we had you both married to each other!'

'We're romantics at heart, Miss Selby,' Mr van Ruyter said, laughing. 'We trust you were not made unhappy by the revelation that he had a fiancée?'

Tamsin congratulated herself once again on how well she managed such a carefree laugh. 'Holiday romances never persist, do they?' she said, forcing a smile. 'They don't really mean a thing. I'm sure Mr Brand knew I realised that when he offered to take me around.'

'That's good,' said Mrs van Ruyter, looking relieved. 'You know, we were quite worried on your behalf. Incidentally, we met Mr Brand this morning and he told us he was on his way to his villa and would be away for a few days. He wished us a good journey.' They went on their way, saying a warm goodbye to Tamsin, too.

So Sarne had gone to his fiancée and would be spending a few days with her, perhaps relaxing after his tiring ordeal as an interpreter. Perhaps, and the thought sent a whiplash of pain around Tamsin's body, he was even arranging his wedding date.

In her room she stood by the window through which they had watched the dawn rise. It was not difficult to relive those moments in his arms. It was all too easy to recall his kisses—which meant nothing; his passionate words—which had meant even less.

She turned away and listlessly turned on the radio, hoping the music would soothe her shattered peace of mind. If it did not mean upsetting her uncle and, as it were, throwing his generosity back in his face, she would leave the hotel that very day and go home. But he might even now be on his way to see her, so she had to stay there at least until he arrived.

It was two days later that the telephone rang in her room. She was on the balcony lying on a sun lounger with her eyes closed—she had no energy or desire to do anything else—and rose reluctantly to answer the call.

'A Mr Williams is at reception, Miss Selby. He has just arrived and would like to see you. Is it possible for you to come downstairs?'

For the first time for days, Tamsin came to life. Her uncle was here, someone familiar and dear, someone to talk to and ask about her parents and her home. As she ran downstairs and saw him standing there, solid, dependable, his cases beside him, his arms outstretched, she could not stop herself from running into them.

'There's my girl,' he said. 'How's life treating you, lass?'

She extricated herself from his bear hug and he looked her over. 'My, you look good, as pretty as ever.'

Tamsin laughed and as she did so, experienced a surge of relief from the unbearable build-up of tension inside her since Sarne had gone away.

Her uncle told the girl at reception, 'Have my cases taken to my room, will you? I'll have a talk with this lass here first. Give me a key, before I forget it. I've got a memory like a bucket with holes in it.'

Tamsin laughed with the receptionist, but she knew that her uncle's memory was excellent, despite his denigration of it. She also knew that under that 'simple man at heart' act which he chose to assume was an experienced, hard-headed man of business.

As they went up in the lift, Tamsin laughed to herself at her uncle's very English approach to everything. He did not know a word of any language except his own and moreover, would boast of it. How he ever made himself understood when he went abroad—as he often did, to one of his numerous European hotels—she could not guess.

They spent over an hour talking about home, about her parents and about the way the hotel was run. She had nothing but praise for it, she told him. Except, she remembered, that sometimes during the day the water was almost cold—certainly not hot enough for a bath. But, she excused the management, if every guest would have a bath or a shower at the same time ...

Her uncle made a note of it, however, and said he'd have to do something about that! He said, 'You're looking a bit pale, love. Are you sure you've recovered completely from that accident? No headaches, no pains anywhere?'

She shook her head. There was nothing wrong with her at all, she assured him. She could not add—except a broken heart. Her holiday had been wonderful from start to finish.

'No need to come home yet awhile,' William told her. 'After all, there's nothing to go home for, is there? No job waiting for you ...'

He looked at his watch. 'I'll go and unpack my bits and pieces, then we must dine together.' He whispered, 'Don't tell anyone who I am, lass. I'll have a good look round. I don't want them rushing about putting things to rights—you know, hiding things from me.'

Tamsin promised to keep his identity a secret. 'Where's your room, Uncle William?' He invited her to go with him, then she would know where it was. Third floor, he said, as Tamsin closed the door behind them. 'We'll walk up.' He patted his middle. 'Exercise will do me good. I'm too fat already, aren't I?'

Tamsin laughed as they went towards the stairs. There was no doubt about it, her uncle's affluence was leaving its mark on him. She thought of her father, brother of the man beside her yet so different from him. Modest in status and position her father might be, but he was still slim and agile.

Tamsin's heart began to thunder beneath her ribs. Coming down the stairs from the second floor was a man, the sight of whom she had been longing for for days. He stopped momentarily at the bend in the staircase before swinging round to the next flight down. He stared first at her uncle and then, narrowly and with deep suspicion, at Tamsin.

He glanced along the corridor where, as he knew only too well, her bedroom was situated. By the cold fury with which he looked at her, it was not difficult to guess the conclusions he had come to.

Now they were within speaking distance. 'Sarne,' Tamsin said, but her voice was strangely timid. The word had been intended as a greeting—a warm, delighted greeting—but it had come out instead as an appeal, a plea for clemency and understanding. 'Don't tell anyone who I am,' her uncle had said. But why, her heart cried out, did that have to include Sarne Brand?

Sarne continued on his downward journey.

'Who was that, love?' her uncle asked, not bothering to keep his voice down.

'Oh,' Tamsin answered as offhandedly as she could, 'a—a guest. Just another guest.'

As he reached the foot of the stairs, Sarne flicked back a look. Tamsin shrank as if his scorn and derision had been a physical thing.

Tamsin dined with her uncle William. For the first time for days, she wore an ankle-length dress, one she had not worn before. It was a dark blue, round-necked and with wrist-hugging sleeves.

Her uncle said it deepened the colour of her eyes and made her look 'so grown-up'. Sophisticated, she supposed he meant. Their table was in a corner and some distance from the table she usually occupied.

Sarne was therefore farther away than before, although Tamsin could see him clearly as he sat alone. Her eyes kept straying towards him and now and then she would catch him watching her. The coldness in his gaze had her biting her bottom lip and playing with her wine glass which her uncle kept filling.

When the meal was nearly over and they had talked themselves into a restful silence, her uncle said, 'Tell me, love, who is it you keep looking at behind me?' And to her horror he turned in his chair and stared straight at Sarne.

'Lass,' his voice was a stage whisper, 'isn't that the young fellow we met on the stairs? The one you called out to?' Was that how her greeting had sounded to him? 'Hey, and what about that young man you told us about on the phone? What's happened to him? Is——' he strained round again, and Tamsin saw Sarne rise angrily and leave the dining-room, 'is that him?'

Tamsin stared at her empty coffee cup. She dared not lift her eyes and let her uncle see the threatening tears. 'He's not a boy, lass, he's a man, a man old enough to be married. Tamsin, love, look at your uncle.' She lifted her eyes. 'You haven't got yourself tangled up with a married man?'

She shook her head. 'He's engaged, Uncle William. He's got a fiancée. She's—she's beautiful.'

'You've seen her?' Tamsin nodded. 'Yes, well,' Uncle William went on, 'you'd expect it, wouldn't you? A man like that, big and handsome, he's bound to have someone ...' He eyed his niece compassionately. 'It's a shame, though. Never mind,' he patted her hand, 'believe me, these things pass. After a while you'll forget and it'll stop hurting.'

But Tamsin knew that the pain she felt now and the agony she would feel on leaving Lugano—and Sarne Brand —for ever would never leave her, however hard she tried to forget.

Uncle William stayed at the Hotel Tranquillité for three

days. He hired a car and took Tamsin sightseeing, even penetrating some distance into Italy.

They were never at the hotel for lunch, but every evening at dinner, Sarne was there. With studied care, Tamsin kept her eyes away from him, even persuading her uncle to change places on the third evening 'for a change of scenery', as she laughingly told him.

'I'm off for two or three days tomorrow, Tamsin,' William said. 'I've seen to my satisfaction how well things are being run here. I'll even praise 'em to their faces! But I won't let on yet who I am.'

Next morning, Tamsin went to her uncle's room to help him pack. He welcomed her assistance. 'I'm useless. Your auntie did it for me when I came, bless her.'

Her uncle left Tamsin while he went shopping for one or two personal items. She opened his cases wide on the floor—they were made of the finest quality leather—and went down on her knees to pack his clothes. Her uncle had left the door open, saying he would not be long. It was a few minutes after he had gone that a feeling crept over Tamsin of being watched.

Her skin prickled, her head turned. Sarne Brand stood at the open door. For a few painful seconds, his ice-cold, contemptuous eyes clashed with hers, then he went on his way. He had told her, scathingly, without words, exactly what he thought of her.

Her head drooped. What had he been thinking? That her uncle was—*not* her uncle? No, that would be too absurd. Why, William was old enough to be her father, anyone with eyes could see that!

Tamsin breakfasted with her uncle. He said, towards the end of the meal, 'How are you off for money, lass?' Tamsin was about to say, I have more than enough, when he produced his wallet and took out a wad of notes, stretched across and put them beside her plate.

'Don't know how much is there,' William said, 'but if

it's not enough, let me know. Now,' he glanced at his watch, 'I must be going.' He stood and bent to kiss her fondly on both cheeks. His hand squeezed her shoulder. 'Look after yourself, love. I'll be back in a day or two.'

He gave a final wave from the door and Tamsin self-consciously pushed the money into her purse. She was aware that Sarne must have seen the giving of the money and the calm acceptance of it on her part. She stole a look at him as he drained his cup.

Moments later, his expression hard, his eyes elsewhere, he pushed back his chair and strode from the dining-room. Tamsin stared through the window at the blurring foliage and flowering plants in the hotel grounds.

The day passed slowly after her uncle had left and Tamsin was back to her loneliness. The hotel had been quiet after the delegates had departed, but now other guests had come to fill the empty places. The hotel buzzed with life and holiday laughter again. But an intolerable listlessness had Tamsin in its grip and nothing she could do—lie in the sun, swim in the pool—would shake it off.

Tamsin was sunbathing on a sun lounger by the side of the pool when she saw Sarne emerge from the hotel and stand for a few moments at the top of the steps. Her heart somersaulted. That was how she had first seen him on her arrival at the hotel. She acknowledged now that even in those first moments she had been ensnared by his dark good looks.

His eyes, which seemed to be seeking for someone, alighted on her. He stared, cold-faced and hard-eyed, at her reclining form, then he swung along the drive. A car roared into life and she knew he had driven away, no doubt to his fiancée at the Villa Magnifico. She stirred restlessly, turned her head to one side and feigned sleep. If anyone talked to her now, she would burst into tears.

That evening, the restlessness was on her again. For dinner she wore a multi-coloured button-through summer dress. If Sarne had come in to dine, she could not tell because she had deliberately sat with her back to the dining-room. She could not bear his contemptuous looks.

Later, she wandered about the hotel gardens, walking between palm trees and exotic plants, under the branches of towering pines. It was dark when she came across the floodlit pool. The lights shining upwards from beneath the surface still intrigued her, and she wondered what it would be like to swim in the glowing water.

Someone, it seemed, had decided to take the plunge because there was a splashing sound as though the swimmer was moving vigorously from one end of the pool to the other. Tamsin emerged from the shadows to watch. It was Sarne.

Fascinated, her eyes were drawn to his glistening body as he stood momentarily at the shallow end and smoothed back his hair. She stayed where she was, despite the fact that her common sense urged her to retreat.

'Tamsin!' He had seen her and she was gripped by panic and could not move. He swam to the side and held out his hand. 'Come here, *cara*.'

Was it true? she wondered, bemused. Had he forgiven her for whatever crime she had, in his eyes, committed? Was his hand extended in a renewal of their friendship? With a muted joy, she ran to the side of the pool. 'Sarne,' she whispered, 'Sarne ...'

She stretched out her hand and it was taken in a fierce grip. Her body unbalanced ... she was falling through the air ... there was a splash of water all round her and she was in the pool beside him, soaked to the skin, gasping for breath. Savage hands gripped her, tearing at her dress so that the buttons pulled apart.

Her hair floated on the water and fingers gathered it, jerking her mercilessly into a floating position. His other hand supported her back and his lips fixed on hers, forcing hers wide and exploring her mouth until she thought she would choke.

Teeth savaged her lips and she cried out as she felt the sharpness penetrate their sensitive skin. He had made her mouth bleed! He released her hair only to touch with a ferocious fondling her breasts which lay revealed beneath the unfastened buttons. His hands ran all over her, her hips, her thighs, her legs, and the clinging material of her dress formed no barrier to his cruel caresses.

'Oh, please, *please*,' she gasped, closing her eyes against the water and the glare of the submerged floodlights. 'Haven't you punished me enough?'

They were treading water now and her hands fastened on to his shoulders for support. She opened her eyes and caught a glimpse of his eyes, hard and blazing in the reflected underwater lighting. Her plea for mercy had passed him by. He pulled her against him full-length, his legs entwining with hers, and she felt his overwhelming masculinity, the rigid column of him against her weakening body.

'Enough?' he muttered. '*Never* will I be able to show you in sufficient strength my contempt for your behaviour. So now I've seen the man who's paying for your keep here, giving you clothes and heaven knows what else. No wonder you denied his existence!'

His hands clamped painfully round her jaw, holding her head above the water. 'What about those wonderful morals of yours, now? "Not my way", you said to me constantly. *Not your way?*' The water ran down his face which, in the illuminated darkness, looked satanic. 'Why else does a man of that age give a girl all he's given you if not for what he gets from her?'

She moaned and grasped his upper arms for support, feeling the whipcord muscles beneath her clinging fingers. 'You're wrong, Sarne,' she whispered, starting to shiver with shock and cold. 'He's n-not my boy-friend.'

'And,' Sarne continued as though she had not spoken,

'while he was many miles away in London, you were here playing around with me. When I threw you aside,' she winced at his contemptuous expression, 'you had to find someone, anyone, to take my place, so you fastened on to those two students. You let them kiss you, as you let me kiss you. Not once did you repulse me.'

She slackened with fatigue, losing her hold on him, and as a result nearly going under. He made no effort to assist her and she floundered, grasping his arm and steadying herself.

'The other night,' he snarled, 'if I had chosen to do so, I could have taken you body and soul and there wouldn't have been a murmur of protest from you. Not only are you easy to get, you're cheap, you're a cheat, a liar and an opportunist. And it's plain to me now I've seen all sides of you that you'd sell your soul—marriage to a man of your father's age—for money and all the comfort it brings.'

'Sarne,' she gasped, almost exhausted but determined now to tell him the truth in spite of her uncle's wishes, 'that man is my uncle, my *uncle*, Sarne . . .'

'And I'm your brother,' he sneered. 'Think of a better title, honey, something more original. How could he be your uncle when your family, if what you've told me about them is true, are ordinary folk, with ordinary jobs and a none-too-plentiful supply of money? It just doesn't fit, sweetheart.' The contempt hit her like a slap round the face.

'P-please, Sarne, I'm cold. Let me g-go.' As he bent to kiss her again, her voice rose and she shrieked, 'Let me *go*!' But she could not evade his lips and the familiarity of his roving hands.

He let her go. It happened so suddenly she almost sank to the bottom. She panicked and struggled and felt she was drowning, but she surfaced, gasping and in distress. Sarne trod water and watched, lifting not a finger to help.

She swam to the steps, climbed them slowly, doubling up

in her breathlessness and taking gasps of air. Then she ran, making for the hotel entrance.

On the way she raced across Sarne's discarded robe, tripped over a sleeve, fell and hit her forehead on the paving stones, crying out at the searing pain which rocketed across the back of her eyes.

Through a mist she heard her name called, heard running steps, felt hands turn her, touch her and lift her. Then consciousness receded completely and she floated away ...

When she regained consciousness, Tamsin thought she was drowning and cried out. Someone said, 'Hush,' and cool, impersonal fingers held her wrist loosely.

'Concussion,' a man's voice said. 'Slight.' Fingers felt her head, turning it gently to one side. 'There is an area where the hair must at some time have been cut away, and not so long ago. There have been one or two stitches in the scalp. An accident probably and possibly also concussion then.' The voice had a faint accent. 'Where is her family?' the voice went on.

'In England.' Surely that was Sarne? Tamsin's eyes fluttered open. 'She's awake.' And the conversation continued in another language. Through the mists which still hung around her mind, Tamsin was unable to identify it, although she guessed hazily that it was Italian.

A man's face bent over her. 'You will be feeling better soon, Miss Selby.' He was grey-haired, Tamsin noticed. 'You have had a bang on the head, but the effects should pass in a day or two. I have given you an injection to help you sleep. You will be looked after. Goodnight, now. I will come again if it is considered necessary.'

Tamsin nodded and found it painful. 'Please,' she whispered, 'how—how much do I——?'

'I'll attend to that, doctor,' Sarne said, and they left the room.

Tamsin tried to think why she was in bed, tried to recall

the events that led up to the present situation. Her brain was too tired, it was too much of an effort ... She slept.

Tamsin woke again. It must have been some hours later because she felt just a little better. She knew by instinct that she was not alone. She stirred and the other person in the room was alert at once.

'Bathroom,' she said, 'please could I——?' Who was it with her? A woman?

A figure, tall and broad, a black outline in the darkness, said, 'You want something?'

Sarne? She couldn't ask *him* ... 'No, no,' she murmured, but the voice said, 'I'll take you there.'

She had no strength to resist. He lifted her and she found she was in her nightdress. Sarne carried her into the bathroom and sat her on the stool. 'Are you sure you can manage?'

'Yes, yes. Thank you.' She looked up, wide-eyed, and saw compassion in his face. She became aware of the soreness of her lip and put up a hand to touch it, remembering clearly now how it had been caused.

'Call me when you're ready.' His eyes did not flicker.

A few minutes later she walked to the bathroom door and opened it. Sarne was angry. 'I told you to call me.' He lifted her and put her back into bed.

'There's no need for you to stay with me,' she said, her voice thin.

He ignored her words and settled on the other bed, covering himself with the quilt. He had not undressed.

When Tamsin woke again, it was morning. One or two of the curtains had been opened and the sunlight was too much for her dulled eyes. Sarne was not there, but she heard sounds of running water from the bathroom.

Her forehead was painful when she pressed it. It felt bruised, but it was not as bad as she had feared. Her lips were still sore and she hoped they were not swollen. When she sat up carefully, the world went round but soon steadied. With her head drooping to rest on her drawn-up knees, she began to make plans.

Today she would go home, but first she must persuade Sarne to leave her. She put from her the thought that she would never see him again. After the way he had maltreated her in the swimming pool and all the terrible names he had called her, it was plain that he hated her. His opinion of her was so low she could not imagine how he had brought himself to stay near her all night.

She lay back and closed her eyes, turning her cheek against the pillow. The bathroom door opened and Sarne emerged, partly dressed, but bare to the waist. He rubbed his wet hair with a towel and watched her as he did so. By the smoothness of his face, it seemed he had shaved, so he must have brought his toilet things from his room. He produced a comb and ran it through his still-damp hair.

Tamsin lay and watched him, hiding from him behind a pale blank face all the emotions he aroused in her. The sight of him behaving in so intimate a manner, as though they were joined in marriage—or a love affair, that love affair he had once declared he would like to have with her—both pained and excited her.

She wanted to get out of bed and press herself to him, wrapping her arms about his waist and feeling the hardness of him against her body. She moved agitatedly on to her side and hugged herself.

He pulled on a short-sleeved shirt and tucked it into the waistband of his trousers, fastening the zip and the buckle of the belt. Her eyes lifted at last to his, a little timidly. She encountered no warmth. So in spite of all that had happened to her at his hands, he had not relented. But had she really expected him to do so? Was this not the 'English' side of him of which he had once warned her to stay clear?

He shocked her by saying, coolly, 'You can't keep your eyes off me, can you? Maybe you would have liked to join me in the bathroom while I took my shower?' She recoiled, but it couldn't have shown because he went on, 'You must have a man around, mustn't you? A male only has to show the slightest interest in you and you're after him.'

Convulsively she hid her face in the pillow. 'I don't know what you mean,' she muttered.

'No? Have you forgotten those two students so quickly?' When she emerged from the pillow to protest, he cut in, 'And myself from the moment you arrived here?' His eyes narrowed and she tensed for the sarcasm. 'I called you a "pet dog", I remember, following me around.'

'That's unfair,' she blurted out.

'I don't think so,' coldly. 'You gave me every encouragement. Not once did you repulse my advances. Yet all the time you had behind you a man, a rich man, who it seems pampers you in every way he can think of—even to the extent of handing over the contents of his wallet, as I saw with my own eyes yesterday morning.'

She tried to defend herself, but she was too choked with misery. She couldn't tell him again, 'That was my uncle.' He would not believe her, no matter how many times she repeated it.

'How long will your—friend be away?'

'A couple of days. So you've no need to worry about me. He'll take care of me.'

'I'm sure he will.' The tone was cynical.

She felt weak, closing her eyes.

'I shall be away today,' he said. 'I'll ask a chambermaid to keep an eye on you. The doctor has ordered that you should stay in bed for the rest of the day. Did you hear?'

'Yes,' with a weary sigh.

'I'll call and see how you are this evening.'

'There's no need.' I'll be gone, she thought.

'Nevertheless I will.' He paused at the door. 'The doctor mentioned something about an old injury. What happened?'

'I—I prefer not to talk about it.'

He shrugged and turned to go.

'Sarne?' He turned back. After this she would never see him again. 'Thank—thank you for staying with me.'

Again that lift of the shoulders. 'Since I was the cause of the trouble, it was the least I could do.'

'Goodbye, Sarne,' she whispered. He looked at her but did not reply. The door closed on him.

She turned on to her front and wept uncontrollably.

CHAPTER NINE

The hours that followed took on the starkness of a nightmare. Politely but firmly, Tamsin dismissed the Italian chambermaid.

But, the girl said, she had come at the request of Mr Brand to look after her because of the fall she had had.

Tamsin had managed a bright smile and pointed to her head. 'It's better, much better, thank you. And so am I. In fact, I'm so much better I think I'll pack my suitcases and start my journey home.'

The girl had looked horrified and tried to remonstrate with her. Signor Brand, he said you must remain in bed. The doctor, he say so, too.'

'But why?' Tamsin had put her legs to the floor. taken a deep breath and raised herself to stand, holding all the while on to the bedhead for support. 'See, I'm quite well, aren't I?'

The girl had looked doubtful and said, 'I must bring you your breakfast. I promised Signor Brand——'

'Breakfast in bed?' Yes, Tamsin thought, she would need all the energy she could muster for the long train journey ahead. 'That would be lovely.'

The girl had beamed and hurried away. Soon a tray was put in front of Tamsin. It contained far more than the customary continental breakfast that was served in the dining-room or on the terrace.

There was a boiled egg, toast, marmalade and honey, fresh fruit, rolls and coffee. 'Wonderful!' Tamsin exclaimed, managing to put a light of pleasure into her eyes. 'If I eat most of this, will you believe I'm feeling better?'

The girl nodded and left her. So Tamsin struggled through the meal, forcing herself to eat at least some of each of the items. Afterwards, she had to admit, even to herself, that she felt a little better.

When the chambermaid returned, she was delighted with the state of the tray. Could she do anything to help the *signorina*? she asked.

'You could,' said Tamsin. 'I'd be very grateful if you'd help me pack my clothes.'

The girl frowned. 'You go away?'

Tamsin nodded. 'Home. I must go to my mother.'

'Ah, your mother!' At last the girl understood. It seemed she could relate to the desire to see one's maternal parent! '*Si, si,* your mother,' she said again, and pulled out Tamsin's cases in a burst of enthusiasm.

When all the packing had been finished and Tamsin was ready to go, she pressed a few of the notes her uncle had given her into the girl's hand. 'You've been a great help,' Tamsin said. The girl had drawn back at the sight of so much money, but Tamsin had insisted and the girl had thanked her haltingly and charmingly.

Tamsin settled her bill and asked reception to call a taxi. At the railway station she bought all the tickets she would need to get her back to London and reserved a couchette in a first-class compartment.

Since the train did not leave Lugano until early that evening, there had been the problem of knowing what to do with herself for the remainder of the day. Somewhere, she thought, where for safety's sake, neither she nor her luggage could be found. Who knew what Sarne might do if he happened to return early and found her gone?

So she decided to spend a few hours on a lake steamer, taking her cases with her. She looked out dully at the beauty of the passing scenery, the intriguing villages, the other craft passing by. At lunchtime, she forced sandwiches and coffee into herself, taking a couple of pain-killing tablets to dull the throbbing in her head.

The sun shone with its customary brilliance and Tamsin found the jacket she had chosen to wear for the journey too warm. As she removed it she saw that on her arm bruises were beginning to emerge, bruises inflicted by Sarne in his fury. She wondered with alarm how other parts of her body had fared under his savage hands and was thankful that most of her surface area was covered by her jeans and shirt. The bruises, she thought cynically, would be something to remember him by. The cynicism did not last. It faded, leaving in its wake pain, and yet more pain. She would never see him again.

When she boarded the train and her luggage had been handed in by a porter, Tamsin sank on to the seat and, now that she was alone, gave in at last to despair. She had the compartment to herself and as the train moved out of the station, the tears ran unchecked down her pale cheeks.

As the distance between herself and Sarne Brand lengthened, a feeling of numbness took over, and she stared resignedly out of the window. It even became possible after a while to give the passing scenery the attention and admiration it deserved.

No one else came into the compartment. At the inquiry office in Lugano, they had told her that, because it was midweek, it should not be difficult to book a couchette at such short notice, although at the weekend it would have been impossible ...

The compartment held four couchettes and Tamsin hoped she would continue to have the place to herself. It was more likely, wasn't it, she reasoned, than if she had chosen to travel in a second-class compartment? With the extra money her uncle had given her, she had been able to buy herself solitude.

She felt no inclination to read, although there was a book in her bag and an English magazine which she had bought at the station. To her relief, as the hours went by, she remained alone. Darkness came, yet still her eyes stared through the window. She noticed dully that the passing shapes of trees and buildings had changed into black shadows. She took care, however, to avoid her own reflection—until there was nothing else to look at.

Then she closed her eyes and the memories came flooding back. Memories of Sarne and his companionship, Sarne and his way of talking and walking, his lovemaking—and his warm, brown eyes.

Memories, too, of a cold, aloof man, who had seared and scarred her with his anger and contempt; of a cultured and clever man with the outlook and bearing of an autocrat but who was at heart warm-blooded and deeply passionate.

A mixture of a man, the like of whom she knew she would never meet again. She hoped his fiancée appreciated the man whose love she had captured, the man who, of all the women he had known, had given her, and her alone, his love.

The attendant came in and informed her, in heavily-accented English, that if she wished for food, there was a buffet car farther down the train. Tamsin thanked him but shook her head and he went away. She tried reading, but it was useless. Her attention kept wandering and she began to wish there was someone to talk to, although unlike Sarne, she would have been unable to communicate except in her own native tongue.

When the attendant returned and told her it was time to pull down the blinds and arrange the couchettes for sleeping, she realised how late it was growing. At Basle, he told her—he pronounced it Basel—the various carriages would be shunted back and forth and gradually all the coaches from trains from other parts of Switzerland which were bound for Calais would be linked to form one train.

Since there was nothing else to do, and since her head ached unbearably, Tamsin decided to settle down in her couchette and sleep. She went along the corridor to the wash-room and washed as well as she could. It was not easy with the swaying of the train and she cut her toilet to a minimum.

Back in the compartment, she spread out the undersheet, unfolded the blanket and pulled it over her. She was fully dressed and the coach was warm. She hoped that the swaying of the train would help her to get to sleep. But sleep did not come. Her thoughts, like her aching head, were too painful. Every turn of the wheels was taking her farther away from the man she had grown, so disastrously, to love.

The speed of the train was slowing, other trains passed at a more frequent rate. Now they had stopped and a voice rang out, speaking in three or four languages, announcing that the station at which they had arrived was Basle. Doors banged, there was laughter and there were shouts. The shunting of coaches had begun and now and then there was a jerk as coaches were detached and others coupled on in their place.

There were footsteps walking up and down in the corridor outside. There came the sound of doors sliding open and Tamsin hoped fervently that no one would come into her compartment. Her hopes were in vain. The door was pushed to one side, fingers fumbled for the main light switch and it came on.

Tamsin rolled on to her side away from the light. She was not in the mood to greet newcomers. She hoped they would see that she had gone to bed and would have the courtesy to leave her undisturbed.

Cases were lifted in. The door slid shut and a voice said, 'Tamsin?'

She tensed, held her breath, then, knowing she was not dreaming—how could she when she had not been asleep?—she turned slowly to look up at the newcomer.

She asked, wide-eyed and in a whisper, 'What are you doing here?'

'I might ask the same of you.' There was an edge to Sarne's voice. 'You've given us the run-around, my girl.' He put his hands on his hips and his legs straddled one of his cases. In the narrow gangway he looked as tall as a giant and almost as frightening.

'You book yourself out of the hotel,' he went on, 'while you're still suffering from the after-effects of concussion. You disappear without trace, baggage and all. Only at the railway station did I pick up any clues. A certain Signorina Selby had reserved a couchette for herself from Lugano to Calais. By the time I stumbled upon this piece of information, I was too late. The train had gone.'

Sarne lowered himself to sit on the case so that Tamsin did not have to strain to look up at him. He folded his arms. 'I had intended returning to the hotel from my villa earlier in the day, but I was delayed. Fortunately, I have a friend who owns a small aircraft stationed at a private airfield. He flew me to Basle and here I am.'

There was a short silence while he studied her face. 'Well,' he said, his expression unreadable, 'what have you got to say for yourself?'

She stared at the base of the couchette above her. 'I don't know why you bothered to come. I left because—because,' she improvised, 'I'd had enough of—of luxury living. I just—just wanted to go home.'

She stole a glance at him to see how he had taken her statement, but his face remained impassive. He rose and hoisted his luggage on to the couchette above.

She lifted herself on to her elbow. His failure to respond angered her. 'So why didn't you simply forget me, the *cheap, cheating opportunist* called Tamsin Selby and go back to your beautiful, faultless fiancée, Nicoletta?' The smile that flickered across his lips roused her even more. 'I'd have gone out of your life. I would have been off your conscience.'

'You may like to know,' he said coolly, 'that I possess a home, too, and that's exactly where I'm going. I have a flat on the outskirts of Birmingham. Also, I felt responsible for you, having been the cause of your present—incapacity.'

He swung a rucksack up to join his cases. Tamsin watched. 'You shouldn't fill those couchettes with luggage,' she said irritably. 'Someone might have reserved them and come in and claim them.'

'They won't. I checked with the guard.'

The colour started to creep into her cheeks. So she would be alone with him for the rest of the long journey. It's unfair, her heart cried out, to torment me like this. Why couldn't he have travelled in another compartment? He didn't care about her, so why did he have to burden himself with the company of a girl he hated? Would he taunt her all the way?

He removed his jacket, throwing it high to join the cases. He loosened his tie, removed it and pushed it into a pocket. Her eyes did not leave him. He was, she knew, aware of her regard, because that maddening half-smile played about his lips again.

This strange intimacy between them was all so familiar, she thought in anguish. How many times had they shared the same room at night?

'Where's the wash-room?' he asked. Tamsin indicated the direction and he slid the door open, shutting it behind him.

She lay back, exhausted. Even his presence stirred her so deeply that she felt drained—and the train had not yet moved from the station on its way to Calais.

She spread her hand over her face, pressing her trembling lips. The thought shot into her mind like a dart in flight. It was still possible to escape. If only she had the energy ...

With a shudder and a jerk, the wheels began to turn and the train was on its way. Now there was no way out. She would have to face the journey, not alone, as she had hoped, but in the company of a man she loved but who she knew hated her.

The door sliding open had her heart throbbing. Her tired body could hardly stand the increased tempo of her blood flow. If she shut her eyes tightly, would he decide that she had gone to sleep?

There came a murmur. 'You look like a child trying to pretend you're asleep.' She opened her eyes and he laughed softly. He crouched on his haunches—the couchette was low down—and gazed at her.

'Will you stop tantalising me?' she whispered, her face white in the poor lighting of the compartment.

'No,' he said with resolution, and stood, reaching up for the rucksack and lowering it to the ground. 'In here I have a flask of coffee and sandwiches, all of which I intend to share with you. I also have some pills given to me by the doctor whose orders you so lamentably disobeyed.' He looked down at her. 'And don't say, like the child you're pretending to be, I won't take them, because if necessary I'll force them into you—and, *signorina*,' his voice turned menacing, his eyes half-closing, 'I have my methods. Now, sit up and eat everything I give you.'

Tamsin swung her legs to the floor and found the action tiring, simple though it was. Her head drooped as she waited patiently. At the first bite of a sandwich, she realised how empty she was, and gladly accepted all the food and drink Sarne gave her. When the pills were handed over, she swallowed those, too, and Sarne dusted his hands like a man who had successfully completed a difficult piece of work.

When everything was packed away, Tamsin yawned and immediately apologised. 'Doctor's pills,' Sarne said briefly. 'But before you drift away, young woman, I think we should have a talk, you and I.' He sat on the couchette across the gangway.

'There's nothing to discuss,' she said dully.

'Ah, but you're wrong. You see, I know it all now. You had your uncle almost frantic—not to mention me.'

'My—my uncle?'

'Your uncle,' he said firmly. 'William Selby, chairman of the company which owns——'

'So you *do* know!'

He inclined his head. 'Everything, including the accident which led to your holiday at the Hotel Tranquillité, the clothes, the money he gave you.'

The relief of his knowing was so great Tamsin closed her eyes.

'He told me also, *cara*, that he thought I meant—something special to you. Is that true, Tamsin?'

She forced her eyes to stay shut. He was an engaged man. If she confessed her feelings for him, it would worry him. After all, during those few days they had spent together, they had virtually agreed to no involvement. If she told him she loved him, it might even embarrass him.

With an immense effort, Tamsin injected a dismissive note into her voice. 'Maybe you did—once. But I got over that long ago.' She was pleased with the bored tone in which she had spoken the words. She turned on to her side away from him.

Rough hands seized her, turning her round. She was lifted out into ungentle arms. His face, a breath away, looked in the dimly-lighted carriage, rugged and harsh, the sensitive mouth tight-lipped and ruthless.

Memories of his brutal treatment of her in the swimming pool returned, but curiously they did not bring with them fear and recoil. Instead, she was swept by a longing to be compelled into surrender, to be forced to submit to the greater strength and uncontrolled desires of the man in whose arms she lay.

When the kiss began, her arms lay loosely across his shoulders. As it progressed and its potency and fire set her alight, her arms tightened round his neck, finding their way to the back of his head, raking feverishly through his thick hair.

Despite her weakness, she felt a new vitality surging through her veins, giving her the energy to respond from her depths, to give kiss for passionate kiss and to demonstrate at last, silently but irrefutably, that she loved him.

Triumph made his brown eyes flash. 'You've told me all I want to know, *cara*,' he whispered.

As he returned her to the couchette, her body went slack. Fingers held her chin, turning her face towards him. 'Well, Signorina Selby,' he said softly, 'where does all this take us?'

She would not look at him, but she could tell by the tone of his voice that he was smiling. Her eyes drooped shut and she seemed to have little control over them. Her depression had returned. He had not denied his engagement, nor had he once said he loved her.

'Sarne, I'm tired, so tired.'

There was a long pause, then, 'Yes, yes, of course. I shouldn't have expected——' He released her and swung her legs on to the couchette. The blanket was pulled to her chin and she lay with her head to one side, her eyes still closed.

There were movements as though Sarne was unfolding his sheet and spreading it wide. The main light was switched off and the other couchette complained under his weight as he stretched full-length.

It was no use; despite the pills, despite the exhaustion,

Tamsin's body would not relax. With the man she loved across the gangway, she could not find rest and tranquillity. The man who, despite the names he had called her and the brutal way he had treated her, had a place in her heart which, even if she never saw him again, no other man would ever fill.

Nor, it seemed, could he relax. Beneath the blinds which had been pulled down over the windows, Tamsin could see the lights of towns and villages flashing by. Now and then a train would pass in the opposite direction. Still Sarne moved about and it seemed that, like her, he could not sleep. Was he hating so much having to share a compartment with her?

'Tamsin?' The light over her couchette was switched on and he was crouching beside her again. 'What is it? Can't you tell me, my love?'

What was he saying? Had he called her his love? It made a mockery of the words. She hid her face against the pillow. 'What's the use?' she mumbled. 'You belong to someone else, to the girl called Nicoletta.'

'*Cara*,' he said softly, 'I think it's time you knew everything, too.' He leant across and took her hands. 'Look at me.' She complied. 'I have no fiancée. Nicoletta, my cousin by adoption, doesn't love me. She never has, nor I her.'

The world started spinning as Tamsin tried to take in what Sarne was saying.

'It was my aunt,' he went on, 'who wanted us to marry. To that end, she told everyone in my cousin's hearing what she longed for, hoping that by uttering the words, she would make them come true.'

He dropped her hands. 'I had to disappoint her. I had the task of telling my aunt today—no,' he checked the time, 'it's past midnight, so it was yesterday—that Nicoletta loved someone else. He's a member of the small dance band which played at La Cantina, the nightclub I took her to so that she could see him. The nightclub which you, you minx, also went to with those damned young students.

'Nicoletta couldn't find the courage to tell her mother, so yesterday I had the doubtful pleasure of telling my aunt and, afterwards, calming her down. She was eventually reconciled to her disappointment and the young man, Angelo, was introduced to her. I left my cousin Nicoletta deliriously happy.'

He straightened and pushed his hands into his pockets. 'The Villa Magnifico was my mother's,' he went on. 'She was born there. The villa has been in the family for a very long time. When my mother went to live in the States, she gave the villa to me. I had no inclination to live there, and in any case, I work in England. So I allowed my aunt—my mother's sister—and my cousin to live there and take charge of the place. When Nicoletta marries, she and her husband will live there, too.'

He crouched down again. 'So now, my sweet, you know it all.'

'So——?' Tamsin whispered, her hopes soaring.

'So I'm free—and yet not free. I'm hopelessly in love.'

Her heart throbbed painfully. His arms found her body in the darkness and it trembled in his hold.

'*Cara*, if I tell you again what I told you that night we watched the dawn break over the mountains, will you believe me? You drive me crazy, girl.' He spoke quickly and ardently. 'I desire you. I want you with every fibre of my being. I want to make you mine for all time. I want us to be as one, my own, my darling ...'

He was there beside her and they lay side by side. His arms strained her to him and she yielded with joy. His lips, tender yet demanding, fastened on to hers. When, with the deepest reluctance, their mouths parted, he whispered,

'Tell me, beloved, tell me in words that you love me.'

'Oh, Sarne,' she whispered, 'I love you so much I——' Tears choked her and she could not go on.

'Hush, my darling. Cry if you must.' Soon she lay spent

against him and his hand stroked her hair. 'Never again will I give you so much pain, not with my hands or my words. The other night in the pool you came up against the passionate Latin side of me. I was mad with jealousy, my love. I may be a cool Englishman on the surface but, sufficiently aroused, my passions take over.'

Tamsin laughed softly, rubbing her face against his chest. 'Yet you warned me against the Englishness in you, not the Latin passion.'

'I was wrong. I should have told you to beware of arousing my deepest emotions, because it was those that did the damage.'

They lay quietly together, listening to the clatter of the wheels and feeling the swaying motion of the train.

'I only managed to contact your uncle because he had left his address and telephone number with reception, in case of emergency. After I had had a long talk with him—he's in Paris, did you know?—he gave me your parents' telephone number in England.' His voice deepened. 'I talked with them and I have your father's official permission to marry you. Have I yours, my love?'

She answered him with kisses.

He said, and his smiling tone robbed his words of arrogance, 'But with or without permission, I would have married you. When we arrive back in England, we'll call my mother in America. Then we shall go to your home. With all possible speed, we'll be married. I refuse to wait any longer for you. I made up my mind from the start that you were going to be my wife.'

Tamsin laughed. 'I always thought you were an autocrat to your fingertips. I was right, wasn't I?'

'Really, my love?' He pretended to be annoyed. 'And how did you come to that conclusion?'

'By the way you stood at the top of those hotel steps, by the way you talked and walked...' She yawned again and her body went slack. 'When I left the hotel and thought I'd never see you again——' She stopped. 'It's too terrible to think about, Sarne.'

'Then don't, my darling,' he whispered, pulling her closer. 'Sleep safely here in my arms. There will be no more partings. For the rest of our lives, we shall welcome each new dawn together.'

Best Seller Romances

Next month's best loved romances

Mills & Boon Best Seller Romances are the love stories that have proved particularly popular with our readers. These are the titles to look out for next month.

A PLACE OF STORMS Sara Craven
THE INDY MAN Janet Dailey
ROMAN AFFAIR Rachel Lindsay
A TRIAL MARRIAGE Anne Mather
LAIRD OF GAELA Mary Wibberley
THE PASSIONATE SINNER Violet Winspear

Buy them from your usual paperback stockist, or write to: Mills & Boon Reader Service, P.O. Box 236, Thornton Rd, Croydon, Surrey CR9 3RU, England. Readers in South Africa-write to: Mills & Boon Reader Service of Southern Africa, Private Bag X3010, Randburg, 2125.

Mills & Boon
the rose of romance

Romance on your holiday

Wherever you go, you can take Mills & Boon romance with you. Mills & Boon Holiday Reading Pack, published on June 10th in the UK, contains four new Mills & Boon paperback romances, in an easy-to-pack presentation case.

Carole Mortimer	— LOVE UNSPOKEN
Penny Jordan	— RESCUE OPERATION
Elizabeth Oldfield	— DREAM HERO
Jeneth Murrey	— FORSAKING ALL OTHER

On sale where you buy paperbacks. £3.80 (UK net)

Mills & Boon
The rose of romance

Best Seller Romances

Romances you have loved

Mills & Boon Best Seller Romances are the love stories that have proved particularly popular with our readers. They really are "back by popular demand." These are the six titles to look out for this month.

THE WIDOW AND THE WASTREL
by Janet Dailey

Elizabeth Carrel was not a 'Merry Widow' but a quiet one; it was so long since her young husband had died that she was content to live an uneventful domestic life with her little daughter. Until her husband's brother Jed came on the scene, to disturb all her peace of mind. After Jeremy's undemanding ways, how could she possibly cope with this forceful black sheep of the family?

GIRL FOR A MILLIONAIRE
by Roberta Leigh

'You'll be Cinderella with a clock that won't strike twelve for three whole weeks!' Christine assured Laurel when she persuaded her to come with her for a cruise in the Mediterranean on a millionaire's yacht. But this, Laurel soon found, was a rather rosy-coloured picture of it all – and when she met Nicolas Ponti she began to wish she had never come . . .

Mills & Boon

BORN OUT OF LOVE
by Anne Mather

Charlotte had married Matthew Derby eleven years ago, to give her baby a father – after Logan Kennedy had deserted her. Now Matthew was dead, and Charlotte had met Logan again and realised that the past was by no means dead. And that Logan attracted her as much as ever...

PASSIONATE INVOLVEMENT
by Lilian Peake

Lucky Tamsin – in Switzerland, spending a long holiday in a luxury hotel, *free* – and with a most attractive man paying her all the attention she wanted! But of course there was a snag – a big one. For she knew that Sarne Brand had completely the wrong ideas about her – and she was not at liberty to tell him the truth. How could the affair end in anything but unhappiness?

STORM OVER MANDARGI
by Margaret Way

Toni had left her job and a go-nowhere romance to join her brother on Mandargi, the cattle station which he managed. She hadn't met the owner, Damon Nyland, but had heard enough about him to determine that she at least wasn't going to fall on the great man's neck when he finally condescended to visit them!

LOVE IN A STRANGER'S ARMS
by Violet Winspear

Arabel had woken up in a hospital in Spain to find she had lost her memory. She knew nothing except what the mysterious Don Cortez Ildefonso de la Dura chose to tell her – and he told her she was his wife! And how could she be sure he was telling the truth?

the rose of romance

How to join in a whole new world of romance

It's very easy to subscribe to the Mills & Boon Reader Service. As a regular reader, you can enjoy a whole range of special benefits. Bargain offers. Big cash savings. Your own free Reader Service newsletter, packed with knitting patterns, recipes, competitions, and exclusive book offers.

We send you the very latest titles each month, postage and packing free – no hidden extra charges. There's absolutely no commitment – you receive books for only as long as you want.

We'll send you details. Simply send the coupon – or drop us a line for details about the Mills & Boon Reader Service Subscription Scheme.

Post to: Mills & Boon Reader Service, P.O. Box 236, Thornton Road, Croydon, Surrey CR9 3RU, England.
*Please note: READERS IN SOUTH AFRICA please write to: Mills & Boon Reader Service of Southern Africa, Private Bag X3010, Randburg 2125, S. Africa.

Please send me details of the Mills & Boon Subscription Scheme.

NAME (Mrs/Miss) _____ EP3

ADDRESS _____

COUNTY/COUNTRY _____ POST/ZIP CODE _____

BLOCK LETTERS, PLEASE

Mills & Boon
the rose of romance